MISTRESS GRIM

MISTRESS GRIM

jane redd
usa today bestselling author

Copyright © 2017 by Jane Redd
Print edition
All rights reserved

Mistress Grim was previously published in the Shattered Worlds Boxed Set (August 2017). No part of this book may be reproduced in any form whatsoever without prior written permission of the publisher, except in the case of brief passages embodied in critical reviews and articles. This is a work of fiction.

Interior design by Cora Johnson
Edited by Haley Swan and Lisa Shepherd

Cover Designer: Christian Bentulan and Rachael Anderson
Photography & Creative Direction: Irvin Rivera
Model: Dana Moore
Makeup: Sifa Sitani
Hair: Cherry Pentenbrink
Photo Asst: Alana Majors & Phil Limprasertwong

ISBN: 978-1-947152-23-6

Published by Mirror Press, LLC

WRITING AS JANE REDD
Solstice
Lake Town (Solstice #2)
Mistress Grim

WRITING AS HEATHER B. MOORE
Heart of the Ocean
Power of the Matchmaker
Love is Come
Condemn Me Not: Accused of Witchcraft
The Tangerine Street Romance series
The Newport Ladies Book Club series
A Timeless Romance Anthology series
Timeless Regency Collection
The Aliso Creek series
The Falling series

MISTRESS GRIM

The Mistress of Death discovers that hearts never truly die.

The Grim Reaper has been collecting souls of the dead for hundreds of years, but even the Master of Death has to pass on his reign. Unfortunately, his progeny is not quite ready to replace him.

Cora Grim, daughter of the Grim Reaper, is suddenly thrust into her father's role. Leaving the Underworld on her own to bring back the dead souls, she discovers that the Master of Death neglected to tell her one thing. She can still fall in love.

One

I have known from the day of my seventh birthday that I was in training as the harbinger of death. For you see, my father is the Grim Reaper.

"Cora," he told me when I was but a child of seven. "One day, you will rule the Underworld. One day, you will replace me."

I stared up at him, my giant of a father with his broad shoulders, powerful arms, and elegant fingers with their black nails. He wore his long, dark hair tied back from his angular face so that his black, black eyes seemed like hollow things against his pale face.

How could I replace my father? In any task? He ruled the Underworld as king. He held the lives of all mortals in his grasp. He could take away the breath of the living with a single touch.

He was called Lord of Death, God of the Underworld, Hades, the Grim Reaper . . .

But to me, he was Father.

He's a father who visits me in the early mornings,

after his nights spent above ground, and tells me tales of ancient civilizations. We sit in my room of color, surrounded by things that every girl likes: butterflies, swans, unicorns. The butterflies and swans are real. Even unicorns aren't real in the Underworld. My bedroom is as large as an earthly house. In the center is a pond where my pair of white swans swims, and my atrium contains butterflies and hummingbirds. The Underworld is not a place of dark and shadows or pools of fiery lava, with cloven-hoofed, half-naked men running around. No, the mortal children's storybooks are just that—fables.

"Cora," a deep voice whispers through me because my tutor is calling me through his mind. "Lessons start at high noon."

We were mind-connected on my twelfth birthday. Master Swan has overseen all my education in order to prepare me to become queen of the Underworld. Master Swan is also my father's brother and would be next in line as Lord of Death but for me.

My name on his lips sounds like a curse word, just as my birth was surely a curse on his life.

I answer, "I am on my way."

I leave my bedroom and start walking down the blue corridor. The Underworld palace is divided into sections according to color. My father lives in the red section, Master Swan in the purple section, dining takes place in the yellow section, all entertainment in the orange section, education and training in the brown section. Children live in the blue section. This includes me.

Although, at the age of nineteen in earthly years, I am no longer a child.

My body has become a full woman's, which is another case that Master Swan has made against me. Women are not as safe as men on earth. There will be more risk for me to enter into mortals' homes. I may be captured, or worse.

A tall and broad male reaper, like my father, will have no trouble imposing fear upon any who might confront him. Not everyone who is dying goes willingly. And sometimes another mortal might try to interfere.

Some might even meet an early demise if they try to interfere too much.

Hence the scythe that my father carries. I have been training with a smaller, lighter scythe. With advances in weaponry, the scythe has become much more "female friendly," although my father prefers his ancient, heavy one.

An errand child in a blue uniform bows to me as I pass by him. The boy's name is Rain, and he always wears a smile. "Hello, Rain," I say. He grins, then scurries off to his tasks. I have never felt comfortable with others bowing to me, but it has been a part of my life since I can remember.

When I leave the blue corridor, I cross the commons, moving around the massive water fountain that reaches two stories high. Three women guard the fountain, wearing their filmy robes of pale rose and tangerine orange. The sirens look identical with their honey-gold hair and blue, blue eyes. On the outside, they appear as the fairest maidens a storybook could ever describe, but their teeth and nails are full of deadly venom. They protect the Fountain of Youth from thieves, both from those inside the Underworld and from those who break into our realm.

At the age of twenty-one, I will begin a regimen of drinking from the fountain once a year. And then I will remain forever twenty-one in my appearance.

The thick wooden door of the purple corridor stands open as I approach, which means that Master Swan can hear me coming. I cross the threshold, and immediately I feel a chill. The temperature in the purple wing is much cooler, and as I walk I pass a row of floor-to-ceiling mirrors.

Today, I wear my usual blue color. When I go through the Mistress ceremony and become queen, I will be able to wear any color I choose. I have already decided to choose red like my father. I will never choose purple because of the association with Master Swan, and I have tired of blue—the color which I've worn my entire youth. My bronze-colored hair falls below my waist, and on most days I plait it away from my face. My eyes are the color of my mortal mother's—pale green. At least so I've been told. I can only rely on the painting of her that hangs in my sleeping room. I am tall, like my father, and I match his olive skin tone.

A door to my left creaks open, and my heart rate jumps a notch.

"Cora," Master Swan says, offering one of his flourishing bows. He's a thin man, only slightly taller than me, and looks nothing like my father. Master Swan's features are pale, his hair white blond, his eyes an amber brown. "We have much to do today—you know better than to dally."

I am right on time for my lesson, but I do not point this out. If there's one thing Master Swan loves to do, it's to contradict me.

Today we will complete the level C anthropology course, but when I see the thick, leather-bound book upon a low table, open to an illustration of a dissected flower, I slow my step.

"What is this?" I ask.

Master Swan comes to stand beside me. "Your father has asked that you learn about the biological reproduction process."

My skin heats beneath my blue shirt.

I refuse to go through a reproduction lesson in my uncle's presence. I have discovered all that I was curious to know in my own research in the library, where every book published on earth is duplicated.

I turn toward Master Swan. Standing so close to him makes me realize that I am now nearly as tall as he. "I have all the knowledge necessary," I state.

Master Swan bows, which only irritates me more. He does this when he disagrees with me, and I take it as mockery.

When he straightens again, he folds his hands in front of him. Another irritant.

Just before he's about to lecture me as to why I must obey all my father's commands, the ground beneath our feet rumbles. I grasp the table to steady myself. The Underworld jolts and rumbles from time to time, similar to an earthquake upon the earth. It's the Underworld's message that something has gone awry.

My uncle rushes to the door and pushes it open.

I hurry after him and stop as I listen to a messenger calling throughout the corridors.

"The king of Navarre has been killed," the messenger calls out. "An emergency planning meeting has been called. All directors report to the throne room immediately."

I freeze as the news sifts through my mind. The king of Navarre, Leopold, is a tyrant on his best days. His crusades have been responsible for killing thousands of unbelievers. His wife has been barren these past eight years, and the king's brother Antoine II has tried to steal the throne from Leopold more than once.

It will be my father's task to travel above our world and bring the king's soul before the Fates for his Judgment. The junior reapers are commissioned to bring the lesser mortals to their Judgments. But only the king of the Underworld can bring in earth's royalty.

I move into the corridor, but my uncle grabs my arms and stops me. "Cora," he says. "Your father wants you to meet in his private conference room. He knew this attack was coming and told me that we need to meet with him once the announcement was made."

I find myself running down the corridor, not waiting for my uncle. I hurry across the commons and into the red corridor where my father's private conference room sits. I am not yet queen, but I have sat in many private councils. And I know that my father will need me.

As I enter the room and find the chair where my father usually sits at the long, red oval table empty, I stop. In fact, all the eight chairs are empty.

The doors to the conference room snap closed as if pushed by a gust of wind.

And something like laughter echoes behind me.

I turn slowly to see my uncle, Master Swan, standing within the room, holding my father's curved scythe—the only weapon that can kill me.

Two

Prince Antoine Leonardo III heard the clopping hooves of an approaching horse, signifying that he'd been found at last. He wasn't surprised that he'd been discovered, only that it took them so long. He left the warmth of the fireplace to throw open the doors of the hunting lodge. No, he had no servants to perform such a menial task. In fact, the only person in his current employ was Mistress Bavare. She cooked his meals and then disappeared, as she should.

Leo had dismissed all his guards and servants as soon as he returned from the final battle over the kingdom of Navarre. His uncle, the king of Navarre, had died three days previous in the great battle. Leo had seen the man's body for himself. Leo's own father, Antoine II, had defeated his older brother after a long two-month siege.

Leo's own part in the battle had been short and victorious. His father had refused to let him fight, saying that the sole heir to the throne did not need to put his life at risk. Leo had fought anyway, much to his father's displeasure. But what good was learning the art of warfare for nearly two decades and never putting it to use? Besides, he determined to shadow his father to ensure the man didn't die. The last thing that Leo wanted was to become the next king. If his father defeated the king of Navarre, then his father would be the next king. Which put Leo as the direct heir.

Leo had always known that he was an heir to the throne of Navarre, but he had never cared. This reluctance on his part had been the great divide between him and his father. Unlike his father and uncle, Leo was not a bloodthirsty warmonger. He didn't care how people worshipped their god. And he didn't think a monarch should dictate religious practices to his people.

Yes, Leo had fought. He'd slain men in the name of protecting his father. And once the battle was over and the king of Navarre declared dead, Leo had left the bloody field heaped with bodies. He'd walked away from his father's victory speech and made his way to the king's hunting lodge. Here, he dismissed the servants who were now having to switch their loyalty to the new king, and Leo tended to his own wounds. Scrapes, bruises, and one small gash that he easily stitched.

Now, freshly bathed and clothed, he stood upon the threshold of the hunting lodge.

The rider was coming fast, and within moments, the

horse and the man atop appeared around the copse of trees.

If the rider was surprised to be met and greeted by the prince himself, the rider showed no surprise.

"Your Highness," the messenger said when he neared, reining his horse to a stop and speaking in a wheezing voice. "I've brought a missive from the new king . . . long may he live."

Leo bit back a scoff. Had his father already declared himself king when his brother's body was not yet cold?

But Leo didn't scoff. If there was one thing that he was good at, it was hiding his emotions. He reached for the sealed parchment paper and tugged it open. There, scrawled in hasty writing, were the words that Leo knew had just changed his life for the second time in as many days. The letter had certainly come from the royal palace, but the news was most unexpected. Leo scanned to the salutation first—it was from his mother.

Son, I am writing in all haste and request that you travel to the palace of Navarre immediately. Your father has ordered a series of celebrations that you must attend so that you can be recognized as the sole heir. Alas, your father has sustained an infection from a wound delivered by your own uncle. The physicians are bleeding him now, but he is so pale. I fear for his life. And if, God forbid, he dies, you will then become the next king.

~Mother

Leo read through the words again, and then a third

time. Finally, he looked up at the messenger, who still sat atop his horse, awaiting a response.

"What is the news of my father's health?" Leo asked.

The messenger's face paled. "He has been injured, that is all I know." The man looked to the letter in Leo's hand.

How had his father's injury become so serious? Leo had watched the battle between the brothers. Leo ran across the field to assist, but by the time he arrived, his uncle had been felled. His father stood over the man, blood dripping from a cut on his cheek, but otherwise looked strong and unharmed.

Leo would have to go to his father and make sure the best physicians in all the land were in attendance. His father could not die. But there was a reason Leo had dismissed the former king's servants at the hunting lodge. The transfer of power was never smooth. The loyal subjects to one king needed time to adjust to the new king. Rebellions might arise and assassination plots might be devised.

"What is the people's reaction to the news of my uncle's defeat?"

The rider hesitated. "They are learning to accept their new king. But your mother recommends you travel with your guard."

Leo had no guard. He'd left the battlefield on his own. He gave a short nod. Traveling back to the palace would be fraught with danger. There were certainly rebel groups and loyalists to his uncle who were already plotting to retaliate and fight against the new king's army.

Once his father recovered, the rebels would be snuffed out quickly, and his father would slowly bring a fractured country under his command.

This had been his father's plan all along. To overthrow the kingdom of Navarre and steal the throne from his elder brother. The dead king had ruled in corruption, giving favors and titles to the highest bidders. Letting the divisive religious groups persecute and torture one another. His father had fought for a valiant cause, but it was *his* cause, not Leo's. Leo didn't want the throne any more than he wanted to live in hiding in a hunting lodge. He wanted to live in peace, on his own land, where he could oversee crops and breed horses. He might have a wife and brood of sons one day who would inherit an estate—not a country or a kingdom.

His father could not die. Leo refused to allow it.

Mind made up, Leo said, "Return to the palace and tell . . . the queen . . . that I'll be there in all haste."

The messenger nodded, reined his horse around, and started galloping away. Leo didn't wait for the messenger to ride out of sight, he was already striding into the hunting lodge. There by the fireplace was the canvas bag in which he'd kept his most treasured possession. He'd been given it in gratitude for saving a man's life. Not just any man's life, but a seer.

Leo had thought the decrepit creature simply a beggar in the streets. Even so, as a young man of sixteen, he couldn't stand the sight of the shopkeeper who was beating the old man with a broom. So Leo intervened, only to find that the old man was nearly starved. Leo had taken him to his townhouse and fed the man, given him a place to sleep for a handful of days, then sent him on his way with his own horse and a satchel of food.

A fortnight later, a bundle arrived with a note attached.

With this cloak, thou wilt become as invisible as a raven at night.
In humble gratitude,
Master Fate

A strange name, Leo had decided. The cloak had appeared well used and repaired more than once. Leo hadn't thought much of it, although he did assume it belonged to the old man he'd saved from dying of hunger. He examined the letter to find an address on the outside: *Beneath the Canal at First Street.* Leo thought it to be the current abode of the old man, although it was in a place unfit for most mortals. Leo had tossed the cloak over the back of a chair and almost forgot about it, when a few days later his valet picked up the thing in disgust. Leo then saw it for what it was. Where the cloak draped in front of the servant's body, everything became transparent, as if there were no cloak nor body there at all.

It took Leo a moment to find his words. "Leave the cloak on the chair," he said. "I'll dispose of it myself." As soon as the valet had left the room, Leo experimented with the cloak, standing in front of his brass mirror.

The article of clothing was remarkable. Anything beneath it became completely invisible.

At first, Leo used it to play pranks, but then his father had started his campaign against the king, and Leo had tucked it away into the bag. He hadn't put it on for over two years, yet he packed it with him wherever he went.

And now he needed to travel through hostile country as the new king's only son.

Leo drew the cloak out of the bag and pulled it across his shoulders. Looking down at himself, he marveled that his lower body and legs had disappeared. He would have to ride his horse bareback so that if someone spotted him, they'd think the horse simply wild.

From the kitchen, Leo grabbed a loaf of bread and hunk of cheese, then wrapped both into the bag. Fortunately, Mistress Bavare wasn't around, and Leo slipped out of the lodge with no one questioning him. He temporarily removed the cloak in order to approach his horse in the stable. He didn't want to scare the stallion.

He urged the horse into a gallop, away from the lodge and toward town, where he rode directly to First Street. If anyone knew how to prevent a new king from dying of infection, it would be Master Fate.

Three

I cannot move for a long moment, for I can hardly believe my eyes. Master Swan, my uncle, and my teacher, is walking toward me, carrying my father's scythe in his hands.

His intentions are clear. And I suppose I should have known this day would come. Still, my heart thumps hard, and my skin is so cold that I think I may have frozen in place. Then my training kicks in, most of it from Master Swan himself. And some of it from my own research, late at night, when the rest of the palace slept.

I take a slow step back and push up my long sleeves. My outfit is not ideal for fighting, but I have no other choice. Quickly I step out of my slippers to get rid of the jeweled heels that will only be an encumbrance.

Master Swan's face twists into an ugly smile—not that I've ever liked any of his smiles.

And then he lunges.

I leap out of the way, my breath already short. He lunges again, and this time I dive toward a heavy chair, then use it to create a barrier between the two of us.

Master Swan only chuckles and brings the scythe down upon the chair. The wood splits in half with a tremendous crack.

"You cannot think you'll succeed," I say in a gasping voice. "Even if you do kill me, how do you expect to defeat my father?"

"The colors of his guard have changed," he says in a calm voice. "When I'm declared the only living heir to the throne, they will rise up in support. Of *me*."

I gape at him. If what he says is true, Master Swan has created a rebellion within the ranks of the Underworld. This means that upon my death, the guards who'd once been faithful to my father will turn their cloaks from red to purple.

I dodge my uncle as he lunges toward me again. All the while I am looking for a weapon. Nothing will defeat the scythe, so I need to outwit him. But he has cleared the room of the artifacts that used to hang on the walls and sit on the tables. There is nothing for me to use to defend myself.

During my first weapons training class, Master Swan gave me the best advice he could give a half mortal like myself. "Never be caught unarmed."

I took it to heart, and at this moment, I'm grateful that I did.

As my uncle skirts the table which I shoved in his path, his chuckle low and raspy, I withdraw the poisoned dagger I keep strapped to my calf. To an ordinary observer, the dagger looks small and quite harmless. But I have dipped it in venom three times, letting it dry between each application. Mixed with blood or other liquid, the venom will regenerate.

Master Swan's eyes widen only slightly, but then his smile turns coy. He isn't afraid of a tiny dagger. A small cut is nothing to whatever his larger plans are for me.

I throw the knife at Master Swan just as the outer door opens.

My uncle leaps out of the way of the knife, but I have prepared for this possibility and have thrown off-center so that the knife grazes his forearm. It may, or may not, be enough.

The door reveals my father and two guards.

"Ha!" Master Swan says. "We've been expecting you, Grim."

"What have you done?" my father growls out, his gaze darting to me, then back to his brother.

"I've only been doing what's been done before," Master Swan purrs. "Usurping authority."

My father lunges for his brother, and the two of them tumble to the ground, the scythe skittering to the floor.

"Take it, Cora!" my father shouts. "Take it! You must transport the new king of Navarre, who is dying now. Hurry to the portal before the junior reapers seal it."

I have questions but do not have time to ask them. I scurry toward the long knife as the two immortals wrestle each other on the hard floor. I've no doubt that my father will defeat his brother. If nothing else, the guards he brought will ensure it. But I don't look back as I race out of the room and run down the corridor. The portal sits in the throne room, in a place that is protected by junior reapers so that others in the Underworld can't transfer to earth and create havoc. I need to get there before word gets out that I am taking over my father's duty. I will be detained because I have not undergone the formality of the transfer of the Grim Reaper title—a title reserved only for the king or queen of the Underworld.

The throne room is filled with courtiers and servants and junior reapers. When they see me enter, their voices hush. I must be a sight to behold. My clothing torn, the scythe brandished in one hand, and my long hair come undone.

"Clear out!" I command. "On the order of Master Grim, I demand that you leave this room!"

Several of the courtiers hesitate, but no one is interested in arguing with the heir to the kingdom, especially when she is holding the scythe of immortal destruction.

As the door shuts behind them, I lift the cross brace that will be a temporary bar against anyone entering the throne room. It will buy me time since I don't know how long I have before Master Swan's turncoats break into the room.

I dash to the wall of tapestries. I lift the middle tapestry and enter a hidden door. Inside the narrow space behind the wall, I reach for my father's cloak in the darkness. It is where he showed me once, and the soft wool smells of his musk and spice. The garment is too big, of course, but I draw it across my shoulders and pull the hood over my hair. I close my eyes, holding the scythe with both hands, and whisper the words which I've memorized.

I had not expected to take this first journey alone. I have been trained, and taught well, but I was still months away from actually going above ground. My father was to take me on my first voyage and teach me how to operate in a mortal realm.

At the end of the chant, my breath leaves me first, and then it feels as if I have been turned inside out. There is no pain, just an overwhelming sense of weightlessness.

Moments pass, although I cannot gauge the exact time, and I feel the air warm and grow fragrant. Unfamiliar.

There is light around me as well, and I slowly open my eyes, only to blink against the rising sun cresting over a distant mountain.

I gasp and take my first breath of mortal air—thick, fragrant, moist. I turn slowly, my cloak dragging along the ground as I move to take in my surroundings.

I'm standing in a field of spring flowers. The violet blooms stretch away from me until they reach a thick forest of trees. Insects are buzzing about me, and birds sing their early songs. I have studied the earth my whole life, so although the sights and sounds are new, I recognize them.

And I know that my mission is to bring the new king of Navarre to the Underworld, so that means I have appeared in his realm. Somewhere close by is his palace.

Sure enough, as I lift my eyes above the thick forest, I see the spires of a stone palace. It can only be one thing—the new king's home.

He will be on his deathbed, of that I am sure. And I will use the scythe to separate the man from his earthly life. Once I bring him to the Underworld, he will face the Fates and meet his Judgment. Beyond my duties, I have no interest in what happens after I bring death upon a mortal. Their life and their choices will determine their eternal destiny.

I lift the cloak so that my feet can move freely as I walk through the dew-laden grass toward the forest. I hope to find a path, but if not, I'll forge my own way.

My feet are soon soaked with the morning moisture, and I marvel at the feeling—it is a bit uncomfortable but not entirely unpleasant. The sound of a horse reaches me—it's galloping. Fast. I am not bothered to think about the rider upon the horse, since I know that I cannot be viewed by mortal eyes. And sometimes even the dead cannot see me. My father has told me it is a rare occurrence for a mortal who is dying to see the Grim Reaper waiting in the shadows.

There are stories, of course, children's stories, of the Grim Reaper bearing down on an innocent child or beloved grandmother. But they are only stories. The Grim Reaper only carries out the Fates' wishes. And no one can escape their fate.

The horse is traveling just inside the forest, and it must be on a path, for its speed is thunderous. Though I know I can easily outpace a horse, I pause to watch the approach. I cannot be seen by mortal eyes, but my father has told me that animals and beasts have a greater sense than man. So I crouch behind a thicket as the horse nears.

I was right. There is a rider. But no mortal would guess what I do. Because I can sense the magic that surrounds the invisible rider and know instinctively that whoever is trying to conceal himself is wearing a fate cloak.

Four

Leo gripped the horse's mane as the beast plunged into the forest. The horse had become skittish as they neared the palace, and Leo whispered encouragement to the animal. "We're almost there, boy. I'll get you brushed down and well fed once we arrive."

They turned toward the palace, following the winding path. Leo had never traveled this way. When he'd last visited his uncle, the king, Leo had been a boy of seven. And his family had traveled in a procession of carriages.

The horse tried to rear up as they passed by a thicket. "Whoa!" Leo called out, not wanting to speak aloud, but the horse was being impossible. "Yah! Yah!" he shouted, and the trembling beast started forward again. "Just get me to the palace, boy," Leo continued, speaking more quietly now.

Not until he reached the palace gates would he reveal himself.

His meeting with Master Fate had convinced him of this plan of action.

The man lived in what looked like a hovel at first glance, but inside the home every comfort could be found. When Leo had knocked on the old man's door, Leo had been unsure of what to expect. Would the man even remember him?

The wizened face had peered out at him, and immediately a smile lifted his thin lips. "Come in, come in, boy."

"Master Fate," Leo started, holding up the bag with the cloak inside. He'd taken it off when he arrived at First Street. "I have questions for you about your gift."

"I have been expecting you for a long time," Master Fate said with a nod. He drew Leo inside, where Leo found a cheery hearth, hot tea, and rugs and art from exotic lands.

"My father is dying," Leo began as Master Fate handed him a warm cup of tea. "I came to you because you're the only person I think could help me."

Master Fate didn't say anything for a long moment. "Your father has fought a long, hard battle. For many years. He will not enjoy the fruits of his labor in this life."

At that, Leo set down the teacup and stepped closer. "Please, Master Fate. Tell me what I must do to save his life." He looked around the room frantically, hoping the man had knowledge of medicine and poultices that might dismiss his father's infection.

"Ah," Master Fate said. "I see that you think I am a healer. Your father will be surrounded by physicians and healers enough." He crossed the room and pointed to a small painting. "This is who you'll need to beg."

Leo looked over at the painting, and he almost laughed, although a cold chill was starting to creep through him. Perhaps he'd been wrong about coming to this man's hovel, cozy as it was.

The painting that Master Fate pointed to was of a tall figure clothed in black. The cloaked man stood in the middle of a dying field of brown, and in his hand he carried the reaper's scythe.

"And how . . ." Leo started in a low voice. "How do I beg mercy from a man of fables?"

Master Fate chuckled—a dry, raspy sound. "Wear your cloak, my son, and you will discover that the Grim Reaper is far from fable."

And then he turned his eyes upon Leo, and in them, Leo thought he saw something shift. For when Leo turned his head, he was no longer inside the hovel. He was once again outside, standing on First Street, his horse tethered to the nearby gas lamppost.

Now, Leo urged the horse along the forest paths toward the palace. The animal was no longer skittish and galloped effortlessly.

When the path opened up and neared the road, Leo slowed the horse and removed the cloak. He was now in friendly territory, having passed any potential thieves and thugs. When the guards at the palace gates saw him, they bowed low, having recognized Leo's royal clothing.

As Leo approached, he called out, "I've come to visit my father."

The guards bowed again and opened the gates so that Leo could pass through with his horse. One of the guards directed him toward the stables, and Leo felt the man's gaze on his back as he made his way there. Other servants and guards paused in their early morning tasks in the outer courtyards as Leo rode past.

Finally, he arrived at the stables, and a stableboy came out. The boy's eyes widened, and he hurried back inside the stables. Moments later, an older man with a hunch in his shoulder emerged.

"Your Highness," the stableman said with a bow.

"Can you brush and feed my horse?" Leo said. "I've business with my father."

"Yes, Your Highness," the man said, offering another bow.

Leo dismounted. There were no reins to hand over, so Leo simply strode away before the stableman could ask him any questions.

He hurried toward the palace, passing servants and guards who bowed to him. He marveled that everyone knew who he was, although he did look quite a bit like his father.

Another set of guards opened the palace doors as he approached, and Leo stepped into the massive stone hallway. Arches extended above him, and large tapestries of hunting scenes decorated the walls.

"Antoine!" his mother's voice echoed in the dimness.

No matter how many times he told her to call him Leo, she insisted on calling her firstborn and only son Antoine. She descended the grand staircase in her velvet brocade dress of deep purple, and she definitely looked like a queen.

"Mother," Leo greeted, crossing to her as she reached the base of the steps. He took her hands and kissed each cheek. His mother's usually rouged cheeks were pale, and deep circles swept beneath her eyes.

Was he already too late? "How's Father?" Leo asked.

His mother burst into tears, and Leo pulled her into his arms, holding her tightly as she cried against his shoulder. Whatever servants had been present seemed to melt into the shadows and leave the main hall.

Leo's heart pounded as his mother cried. Was his father already gone? Would Leo be declared king by a bruised country?

When his mother's tears abated, he drew away and said in a gentle voice, "Take me to him."

His mother nodded and gripped his hand, and they started up the stairs together. Leo didn't have the heart to question her further, so it was with dread that he pushed open the door to his father's chambers.

A large bed stood in the center of the room, across from a grate with a roaring fire. The room was stifling and smelled of thick incense. The newest king of Navarre was propped up by pillows. His face seemed thinner, almost gaunt, but his eyelids flickered open as Leo approached with his mother. The new king was alive, and that was all that mattered to Leo right now.

Relieved, he stepped up to the bed and grasped his father's hand. He leaned down to kiss the man's brow and said, "Long live the king."

His father's face twisted into a faint smile. "Son, you're here."

"Yes." Leo scanned the others in the room. A couple of the men wore physicians' robes, and a younger lad looked like an errand boy. A woman stood in the corner, past the tall windows, wearing a cloak that concealed her face and most of her body. She seemed about Leo's age, perhaps a year or two younger. Something jolted through Leo at the sight of her. Who was she? One of his mother's handmaids?

His father spoke again. "How was your journey?"

"Uneventful," Leo said. He didn't share his visit to Master Fate or how he used the cloak in order to pass border patrols that might not be so accommodating to the heir of the new king in a defeated country. "Tell me about your illness. What has been done to heal you?"

His mother stepped up then, her tears dried, her breathing steady, as she told Leo about the bleeding, the poultices, and the incense burned in the room.

Leo nodded at her explanation, but his gaze was drawn again to the woman standing beyond the windows in the corner where the draperies met the floor. The sun had begun its morning journey, and the sunlight sparkled against the mottled glass windows. The rays that touched the hem of the woman's cloak seemed to morph from golden orange into an almost transparent violet. *Very strange,* Leo thought, but he didn't have time to demand an introduction or explanation for a woman who was surely his mother's servant.

Still, Leo found his skin growing prickly in the heat of the room, and he started to sweat uncomfortably. He drew off his outer coat and draped it over a nearby chair. Then he turned to his mother. "I'll watch over Father for a time so that you might rest."

His mother's eyes filled with gratitude as she lifted up

on her toes and pressed a kiss to his cheek. He could tell she was on the verge of more tears.

"I'll fetch you if I need anything," he assured her.

She nodded, leaned over to kiss her husband, then turned and left the room.

The woman in the corner did not follow.

Leo shook the curiosity off and strode to the windows. The woman didn't move. Leo thought she might step away from him, or even curtsy as was due his position. She simply remained absolutely still. The hood of her cloak kept her face shadowed and indistinguishable.

Leo reached for the latch on the first window and turned it. Then he pushed the pane open. The cool spring air rushed in, bringing Leo immediate relief.

One of the physicians crossed to Leo and said, "We need to keep out the evil spirits and burn them away."

Leo had heard of such theories before, of course. He turned to face the man. "The room is stifling, and I can barely breathe. I've lived most of my life in the country, and I'm healthy."

The physician took a step back, his gaze darting away. "I have treated many a sick man, Your Highness. I believe that—"

"I have heard enough," Leo said. "Make yourself useful, sir, and bring clear broth for my father." He looked over at the other physician, who stood with his mouth agape. "Put out the fire, man, or ask your servant boy to do it."

"Antoine," his father said in a shaky voice from his bed.

Leo held up his hand to stop his father's words. It was a bold move; but Leo would be damned if he watched his father die.

The two physicians went about Leo's bidding, and with another glance at the woman who now stood just a few paces away, Leo moved back to his father's bedside. He drew down the covers that concealed his father's injured leg.

Leo tried not to wince at the red, taut skin that surrounded a deep incision. The gash had been neatly stitched, so at least there was that. But it was plain that the wound was festering. Tentatively, Leo touched the skin surrounding the wound. It was burning hot. His father winced at the touch.

Men had lost their limbs in battle and had survived. Would his father need to undergo something so drastic as an amputation? The air was cooling around him, and it helped Leo think better. He'd hoped that visiting Master Fate would provide him with the answers to help his father. But it seemed the old man had lost his mind and had only told him to wear his cloak and beg for mercy from the Grim Reaper.

The physicians left the room. At least the fire was out, and hopefully one of the physicians would return soon with the broth.

His father closed his eyes, seemingly exhausted by the effort of holding a short conversation with Leo.

Leo glanced over at the woman in the corner. She still hadn't moved. What was she doing? What was she waiting for? Was she some sort of female healer?

The room was presently empty save for Leo, his father, and the woman. "Who are you?" Leo asked.

She didn't move, didn't speak.

Another look at his father told Leo that the king still had his eyes closed and was probably asleep. Leo took a few steps toward the woman. "Are you a physician?"

It was then he noticed something glinting at her side, just concealed by her dark cloak. It shone like metal—the metal of a sword.

Five

I CAN'T MOVE. I shouldn't move, I decide. The prince, named Leo, or Antoine, I am not sure which, is speaking to me. How is that possible? My father has told me that some mortals can see the reaper right before their deaths. And very few mortals who have the sight can also see reapers. But this young man is far from death, and I do not think he has the sight. He radiates life and strength and vitality. Unlike the man in the bed, whose soul is living its last hours on earth.

"Leo" is taller than me by several handspans, reminding me of my father in that way. But he isn't as broad, a sure sign of his youth. I estimate him to be twenty years of age or so. His dark hair is wavy and pulled back into a tie. I can imagine that if the tie were broken, his hair would fall against his shoulders.

I have no doubt this is the man who'd been riding the horse through the forest. I felt his presence then, and I felt it the moment he came into the king's chambers. The stirrings of my attraction to this prince are undeniable, and I have known this was possible since I've been old enough to hear tales of fated mortals and Underworld creatures. They always ended in tragedy and disaster. My own parents are a testament of that.

But I am not prepared for this young prince's eyes and the way they seem to see everything in the room. Even me. His eyes are the deepest blue I've ever seen, deeper than the color of the blue corridor in my palace and the blue clothing I wear. Deeper blue than the depths of the Fountain of Youth. And those depths are staring right at me.

Impossible. Yet . . .

I step forward, and he stops. His eyes widen.

And something strange happens inside of me. My heart races as if I am facing my uncle and the scythe again. Except it's not the sensation of fear that floods through me. I am not afraid this time. I am . . . curious, fascinated. Compelled to speak.

"You can see me?" I ask.

One of the tasks of a reaper, or so my father has told me, is to withhold all speech. I am merely to collect and deliver the soul to the Fates. I am not to answer their questions, address their concerns, or solve their worries. I am to remain silent.

But I have to know.

"Why wouldn't I be able to see you?" the prince says.

My throat feels like it is about to close. Was the message wrong? Was I to bring back this young man and not his father? Will this young man meet his fate in the next few moments? Perhaps an arrow will fly through the window he opened? Perhaps the physician will bring back a poisoned draft for him. Perhaps his heart will unexpectedly give out.

"I am..." I start to say. If there is one thing I am not, it is at a loss for words. But now I find myself at a crossroads. Do I identify myself? Do I warn him? Do I return to the Underworld to find out my true task? And when I do, will I find my father and uncle still locked in battle? The time might pass here in days and weeks, while the time below is only spent in minutes.

I lift my free hand, the hand not holding the scythe, and push back my hood. Perhaps if he can see me, then my bronze-gold hair and immortal eyes will send him warning enough.

Indeed, his lips part as if he cannot believe what he is seeing. Even if there were a mirror close by, I know that I am not visible in earthly reflections as a mortal is. But I am visible all the same.

"You . . ." he begins. "You are not my mother's handmaiden?"

I feel a smile tug at my mouth. This mortal is quite interesting, but naive. "A handmaiden? You mean a *servant*?"

He is staring at me, and his voice is low when he speaks again. "Are you a healer?"

I shake my head. I am the opposite of a healer, but if this mortal is not the next to die and be transported into the Underworld, then I do not think he needs to know any more about me.

And then suddenly the prince steps closer and

touches my arm. His eyes are on the scythe that I hold in my hand.

But the fact that he touched my arm, and that I feel the warmth of his hands through the cloak, causes me to flinch. I know I am of substance, but I have never been in contact with a mortal. My heart is pounding, and all that I can think about is that I need to get away—away from this prince.

"You *are* real," he says in an incredulous tone, dropping his hand. "You're not a vision or a spirit."

"A spirit?" I almost laugh. "I am hardly that."

He is backing away, which is good. I don't think he should have touched me, and it's something I'll have to think about later. This young man must have the sight. I've heard the stories told of other reapers and what happens when they cross paths with a mortal who is gifted with sight. It often ends poorly for the mortal when they tell others they have seen something otherworldly.

For now, I have a job to do. The king's soul is lifting from his lifeless body. I can see the separation from my corner. In another moment my job will start, and I will transport my first soul to the Underworld.

The prince rushes to his father's bedside and speaks urgently to the man, pleading with him, begging the monarch not to die.

"I do not want this kingdom," the prince says.

I am surprised at this statement coming from the king's heir. In all my study of history, the royal families make it their ambition to rise to power, and it's considered a privilege to inherit the throne. Battles are fought and monarchs killed in order for the next heir to take over.

Hadn't this new king just defeated his own brother to claim the throne?

Perhaps this was the prince's way of cajoling his father back to life.

The infection on the king's leg has become a septic thing to his body, yet the king's soul hovers, as if listening to the prince.

Another moment, and I may need to use force to draw away this newly departed soul. The work of the reaper must be timely, for there are other souls to transport.

"You!" the prince yells, turning to face me once again.

I haven't moved from my corner, but I have unveiled the scythe that I carry, ready to threaten the king's soul with it—if that's what it takes.

"You're the Grim Reaper!" The prince is moving toward me, his eyes wild, his skin flushed red. He is still handsome, in an angry, passionate way, and his desperation seems to reach out like long fingers and wrap around my heart.

How does he know who I am? I am equally appalled and flattered.

The prince grows closer, his breath coming in gasps now as he reaches for my arm. Again, he is touching me, again I feel the warmth of that touch race through my body.

"Spare him, I beg of you," the prince says, no longer yelling, but his pleading words still carry every bit of power. "I cannot take the throne. My father has fought his own battles, not mine, and now he will lose his life because of a simple infection." He releases me, then scrubs his hands through his hair, releasing a guttural groan.

I don't move. The soul is still hovering over the king's body. No one else has returned to the room, despite the fact that the prince's cries must have echoed throughout the entire palace.

"You'll be king," I say. "Isn't that what all princes want?"

The prince seems to pause, and his eyes are a little less feral. He is looking at me, really looking at me, as if I am a fountain of water in a desert hundreds of miles wide. "No," he whispers. "I never want to be king. I would rather die first."

I lift a single brow. This prince does not know what he is asking.

"Take me instead," he continues. "If you must take a soul today, take mine."

I consider for a moment. My father has told me of bargains he's struck before. I could take a replacement soul. I could restore the life of the king and in exchange bring the prince's soul with me. But as I gaze right back at him and look into the depths of his blue eyes, I find I cannot grant his wish.

I do not know what my father would do in this situation. I can only follow my own instincts.

Time has run out, and I walk to the bed containing the king's lifeless body. And just as the queen runs into the room, screaming for her husband, I shove his soul back into the cooling mortal flesh.

Six

Leo sank to the floor, feeling as if all the blood in his body had frozen. He couldn't breathe, couldn't move. He watched as his mother bent over his father and grasped his face. Tears spilled down her cheeks as she sobbed. And then she'd buried her face against the king's neck. The two physicians ran into the room and hurried over to the bed. One of them pulled his mother back while the other checked to see if the king was breathing.

"He lives," the physician declared.

Leo blinked.

"He lives!" the physician called out again, triumphant.

Leo's mother screeched and sank to the floor herself, calling praises to the Almighty and anyone else who might be listening.

But Leo knew this was not the work of God or benevolent angels.

It was the work of a young woman with sea-green eyes and bronze-gold hair. A young woman who did not belong in any earthly realm and who carried a sword of silver death.

She had returned his father to life.

And Leo knew that he would pay for it, just as he offered.

"Son, what happened?" his mother asked, grasping his hands.

Leo hadn't noticed that his mother had made her way over to him where he was kneeling on the floor. "I heard you yelling!" she continued. "I thought your father was dead."

Father had died . . . And then the woman restored his life. Leo blinked again and tried to focus on his mother's words. "He—" Leo's throat was too raw to continue speaking.

His mother started weeping again, this time with joy and relief. Leo had never felt so exhausted, through every part of his body and deep into his bones. His limbs felt heavy, but he forced himself to rise to his feet. To cross to his father's bedside. To look past the king's blinking and alert eyes. To examine his father's leg.

The stitches remained, but the swelling had gone down. The tissue around the gash was pale and no longer an angry red. His father was laughing and calling for wine to celebrate his "return from the dead."

Leo merely nodded and stepped away as his mother returned to the king's side.

Leo watched for a moment longer as his parents embraced, both with tears in their eyes. He watched as one of the physicians helped the king to his feet and he took several steps. He watched a man who'd been dead only moments before act as if he'd never been injured in the first place.

And then Leo left the room and all the rejoicing and praising of God. He passed by servants who were rushing to the king's chambers to see the miracle for themselves.

Leo had to find her. He had to find out why she'd left him behind.

By the time Leo had scoured the palace and surrounding courtyards, an announcement about a celebratory feast had been made by a running page: "The king lives! Long live the king! All are invited to the banquet to celebrate!"

Leo ignored any summons as he made his way to the stables. There, his horse waited. Rested, fed, brushed.

The young woman must have traveled to the palace somehow—someone must have seen her arrive, either on foot or on horse. He found the old stable master sitting on a stool, whittling away at a piece of wood.

"Did you board a horse for a young woman today?" Leo asked.

The stableman looked up, his rheumy eyes wide. He got to his feet and bowed. "Yours was the only horse we stabled today, Your Highness."

"What about yesterday, or the day before?" Leo pressed. "Did you see a young woman, perhaps eighteen or nineteen? Long hair?"

"No, sir," the man said. "I can have the boy be on the lookout. Is it a particular lady friend of yours?"

Leo almost laughed. They were far from friends. He didn't even know her name. "No, I am just looking for someone . . . Never mind." He'd searched everywhere in the palace and the grounds. He'd questioned guards, cooks, maids, and all of them had looked at him with confusion. He'd even gone back and spoken to his father's physicians. No one would admit they'd seen her.

Perhaps . . . perhaps she didn't need a horse after all. How did the Grim Reaper travel anyway? Or, in this case, *Lady* Grim?

Leo saddled up his horse using one of the royal saddles the stable master brought from the healthy arsenal. He wouldn't use the cloak unless he needed to, and with his father's recovered health, Leo felt safer.

He just wanted to know why he was still alive.

He'd offered his life in exchange for his father's, but upon the return of his father's life, Leo still had his own as well.

A tightness formed in his stomach—like a warning or a foreboding—at the thought of going after the woman. But it was gnawing at him, and he felt like a possessed man, intent on finding her as soon as possible. He was, he realized, acting like his father. Leo wished he could speak to Master Fate. The old man had been right.

The answer to saving his father was speaking to the Grim Reaper.

Leo just hadn't known that the reaper was a woman—a woman whom he now had to find.

He urged his horse out of the stable grounds and toward the main gates of the palace. There, the guards let him through, probably wondering why the prince was leaving before the king's celebratory banquet.

Once Leo reached the turnoff path into the forest, he slowed his horse and dismounted. If the young woman hadn't come on horseback, she must have been walking. He tied his horse to a nearby tree and started to walk along the path, searching for footprints that might belong to a woman, or any other clues. Perhaps her cloak or dress had snagged on a branch of a thicket. Perhaps she'd grown tired and had stopped to rest.

He trudged along the path, back and forth, until he had covered as much ground as possible before the night set in. He was hungry and tired, but he wouldn't give up until he found her. He'd find Master Fate again and see if he could figure out what exactly had happened. Finally, Leo arrived back at where he'd left his horse to graze.

He would ride through the evening, back to First Street. And this time, he'd demand real answers.

Leo mounted the horse, and as he rode along the path through the forest, his horse became skittish, reminding him of the previous journey to the palace. The horse had been hard to manage.

"What is it, boy?" Leo asked, allowing the horse to slow a bit.

The beast seemed to resist Leo's command of the reins.

The horse jerked beneath him as if he'd stepped on a forest critter, but there was nothing on the path. "Easy, boy," Leo said, trying to keep his tone calm and firm, although his heart had started racing.

And then the hairs on the back of his neck rose, and the air about him seemed to cool suddenly. Leo didn't know why he spoke, but the words were out of his mouth before he could stop them. "Are you there?" he called. "Show yourself."

In truth, he wanted to turn the horse around and gallop all the way back to the king's palace. He'd never been spooked easily, but it wasn't every day that he met a being from another realm.

"Miss?" he said. "I cannot see you, but my horse can sense you."

The horse tried to rear up. It was taking all Leo's strength to keep the beast from throwing him off and bolting.

"If you're here, I demand that you show yourself," Leo said, loudly now. No one was about to hear him, to think he was a mad fool shouting at the trees in the middle of the night.

Something took form on the path up ahead, and the horse bolted forward toward the dark shape.

"Halt!" Leo cried out, trying to rein in the horse, but the beast was possessed with terror. Leo hung on with all his might. If he fell off now, he'd be knocked out cold and probably break more than one bone.

The shape was feminine, Leo would bet his life on it. But just as the horse neared, and Leo was about to catch a glimpse of the woman's face, the shape dissipated. *Disappeared.*

Leo turned his head to look behind him as the horse continued its frantic gallop. The woman was completely gone. Had he been seeing things? Unfortunately the only other witness was an animal that couldn't talk.

Leo leaned into the horse as it continued to run through the forest, both of their hearts racing. Once they cleared the trees, Leo tried to get the horse to slow down, but it continued at its breakneck speed.

So Leo kept hanging on.

First Street was absolutely silent by the time Leo arrived. The horse had finally slowed down and now walked at a measured pace along the cobblestones. Every hoofbeat seemed to echo twice as loud into the still night. Leo felt the animal trembling beneath him, and he knew he needed to rest it.

Once again, Leo knocked on the door to the hovel. No light reflected in the windows, and after a second knock with no response, Leo determined to wait outside the man's door. But then the door rattled and opened.

Master Fate stood there, his robes pulled closely about him and his eyes dark and luminous in the glow of the single tapered candle he carried.

"Your father lives," Master Fate croaked out. "But I am surprised to see *you* alive."

"You knew," Leo said. There was no point in engaging in niceties now. "You knew that I'd have to offer my life for his."

Master Fate gave a slow nod. "It is the way of the universe."

Leo leaned close so that Master Fate would not

misunderstand any of his words. "Why did you not tell me the Grim Reaper is a woman?"

The man stepped back, his gaze skeptical. "A . . . woman?" He pulled the door open wide. "Come in. Hurry!"

Leo crossed the threshold and was surprised when Master Fate shoved him out of the way of the door before closing it tight and locking it.

He set the candle in a sconce on the wall next to him. The room leapt with light and shadows. Master Fate grasped Leo's forearm. "A *woman*, you say? How old was she?"

Leo had not expected this response. "I—I would guess about twenty years of age."

Master Fate dropped his hand and turned away. He moved to the door and braced both hands against it, then exhaled.

"What is it?" Leo asked. He thought he'd felt terror in the forest, but now it was building up again.

"The Grim Reaper has a daughter," Master Fate said in a strained voice. "If she has taken over this early, that means something has gone terribly wrong in the Underworld."

Leo snorted. "The Underworld?"

Master Fate straightened and spun around. "You saw her. Tell me—what did she look like? Did she carry the reaper's scythe?"

"Yes, she carried a scythe," Leo said, and watched as the color drained from the man's already pale face. "She . . . She looked about twenty years of age, as I said. Her hair was long, almost to her waist. She wore it unbound. She was tall. Perhaps only a handspan shorter than me. Her eyes were . . . green. I asked her if she was a healer, or a spirit. She told me she most definitely was not a spirit." He stopped.

Master Fate covered his face and had let out a groan.

"What is it?" Leo demanded.

When Master Fate seemed to collect himself, he lowered his hands. "This young woman—she is most definitely the daughter of the Grim Reaper. And if her father has passed on the scythe to her, that means she is now the queen of the Underworld. You are never supposed to engage a leader of the Underworld in a conversation. To do so is to turn your soul, and all those who you are related to, over to the reaper."

SEVEN

I FOLLOW THE prince. I cannot stop myself, although I know I should return to the Underworld and find out how my father has fared against Master Swan. I have found that mortals on earth travel quite slowly. One of my steps is faster than a dozen of theirs.

The prince sensed my presence in the forest and called out to me. I decided to step onto the path before him, but then his horse went absolutely mad. I do not understand animals; they are less predictable than mortals. So I melted once again into the forest, out of sight.

The prince travels through the forests, across meadows, around small villages. And soon I notice something isn't right—there is more going on than me simply letting the prince live after I restored his father's life.

The air has a rotting smell to it. I know that the scent is too faint for mortal senses. The smell is something that I've learned about but haven't ever actually smelled. So at first I doubt.

When the prince turns onto a main path that connects to a road, I know that he is nearing his destination. The rotting smell grows stronger as we approach a small town.

It is the smell of death—but not of a corpse a day or two gone. It is the smell of a soul trapped inside a dead body.

My throat feels tight at the realization.

There is something terribly wrong in the Underworld if the junior reapers are not doing their jobs. They should be transporting all these souls and freeing the bodies so that the corpses can return to dust.

Instead, for some reason, the reapers have vacated earth, and the men and women and children who have died since the last sun set are prisoners in their own rot.

Now the prince knocks on a door of a small house, and I am curious as to why he came here.

The stench is not strong here, which gives me the small comfort of knowing that there is not a dead mortal within.

The man who opens the door to receive the prince gives me pause. His skin is wrinkled, his body aged, yet he is familiar to me. And then I realize, as the man pulls the prince inside and shuts the door, that he is one of the immortal Fates.

Most of them are gone from the earth now, and the only Fates I've ever seen are the ones who sit at the Judgment Bar of Eternity. But there is no doubt the man at the door is a Fate. The reddish-purple glow of the amulet at his neck is sign enough, not to mention that I recognize his cragged face from my studies of the world.

What is the prince doing here? What are they speaking about? I walk to the door and try to peer through the windows. I can very well enter the house, but I know that the Fate will become aware of my presence if I do so.

I walk around the house, looking for a better watching point, when a voice whispers to my mind.

Master Swan is mind-speaking.

"Your father's reign is over, Cora," Master Swan whispers, his hoarse tone jarring me to my very center. I reach for the wall of the house to steady myself. "He has, finally, been put in his place, and I am now king of the Underworld. You, my dear Cora, must return with the scythe, and I promise that you will be able to see your father one more time. If you do not return and hand over the reaper's weapon, your father will be stripped of his power and banished to the outer realm."

My legs give out, and I sink to the cool, damp ground.

Master Swan has somehow defeated my father. If my father has been stripped of power, the only thing that can restore it is the scythe. As the harbinger of death, the owner of the scythe has the power to rule the Underworld. As long as it is in my hands, my uncle cannot fully claim the kingdom.

I wrap both of my hands around the hilt of the glinting piece of metal. I close my eyes and think of my father, *willing* my father to communicate with me. But we are not mind-connected. What if he is already dead? What if Master Swan is merely luring me back so that he can imprison me and take the scythe?

Today, I have witnessed both ends of power—those who will do anything for it, and those who will do anything to avoid it. Inside the house on the other side of the stone wall from where I lay, a prince who never wants to be a king speaks to Fate. Beneath this earth, in the deep caverns of the Underworld, Master Swan desires all power over life and death.

I release my breath, then fill my lungs with the damp, moist air.

Somewhere a dog barks.

A breeze stirs along the house, lifting a few tendrils of hair from my face. I squeeze my eyes shut as the voice comes again. A new warning.

"You have ten earthly hours, Cora," Master Swan says. "At the end of the tenth hour, it will be too late."

His words bounce around in my head, and I find that I cannot respond to him. I cannot question or rant or weep.

I have no doubt that I will do anything to save my father. But I also know that my father would not want Master Swan to rule the Underworld.

Ten hours . . . ten earthly hours.

The time seems to be sifting through my fingers like dry sand. I must get up, I must move. I must make a decision.

Something warm touches my shoulder. Perhaps the breeze has turned warm. Yet I cannot move, and I have no strength to open my eyes and turn my head.

"Miss," a man's voice says.

At this, my eyes open.

The prince is kneeling by me, his hand on my shoulder. Why does he keep touching me? It stirs up my blood.

His eyes widen as our gazes connect, and he immediately falls back.

"Cora."

I am fully alert now, and I scramble to a sitting position. He knows my name. The Fate must have told him. Sure enough, standing near the corner of the house is the Fate. He watches me with wary eyes—and he should. I see that his amulet is glowing a deep purple, morphed from red. Earth does not like it when two immortals are in close proximity to each other. Already the wind has increased, and clouds are stirring overhead. A faint grumble of thunder erupts. In moments, it will be accompanied by lightning.

My education has been thorough.

I climb to my feet although I want to stay curled up on the ground. I keep the scythe gripped securely in my hand.

The prince's gaze moves down the length of my body to the scythe.

"I must go," I say, and turn to flee this place.

But another voice stops me. That of the Fate's.

"Mistress Grim," he says. "Your father is dying."

I stop, having made it only a few paces away. "How . . ." I turn. "How do you know?"

The immortal points upward, at the stirring sky

above. The edges of the dark clouds are now seeped in scarlet, as if the sky itself were bleeding.

I feel as if my body has turned to stone. The sky is displaying the keening sign. When an immortal loses power, the very heavens grieve. The red scarlet that edges the clouds acknowledges my father's color: red.

My mind swirls, mimicking the churning, dark clouds above. The wind doubles its strength, then doubles again. I press myself against the wall as my cloak and clothing whip against my body. I grip the scythe, afraid that the wind is strong enough to tear it from my hands.

"Come," the prince shouts above the gale. He tugs my arm and pulls me along the edge of the house. I do not want to go with him, but I find I have little choice. In moments, the wind will overpower me.

Lightning crackles overhead, followed by a terrific boom of thunder as the prince pulls me inside the house with the Fate. He slams the door shut and locks it.

I can barely breathe, and it takes a moment for my eyes to focus on the dim interior. Everything is remarkably still after the violent weather outside. Something clatters against the windowpanes on the other side of the door, but the thick glass doesn't break.

The males face me, and I don't wait to question the Fate. "How long have you been here?" I ask, meaning how long has he been living on earth.

He glances at the prince, who nods.

What are they communicating about?

The Fate looks back at me. "I have been here nearly a century. I knew your father a long time ago."

"You left the Judgment Bar?" For he should have met my father on many occasions.

"I was exiled after I lost a debate," the Fate says.

I have heard of exiled Fates before. When the Fates disagree on a soul's Judgment, sometimes it escalates and affects future Judgments. The Fate that is deemed wrong must leave its seat. But I can see the prince is confused at the conversation. Perhaps the Fate can explain to him later. Right now, I must put together a plan to save my father.

"You have your father's scythe," the Fate observes.

"Yes," I say, glancing down at the silver sword that is dull in the dim light of the house. "My father gave it to me so that I could transport the king of Navarre's soul."

The Fate grows silent, and he bows before me. When he lifts his head again, he says, "Your Majesty. I did not realize that the order of the Grim Reaper had transferred to you."

I bite my lip. A rather juvenile thing to do since I am, in name and blood, a queen. "No one knows—not yet," I say. I notice that the prince has taken a step back. He is staring at me with an unreadable expression on his face.

"Come and sit," the Fate says, leading me to a chair that faces a glowing hearth. The small fire is somehow comforting. The Fate sits near me while the prince leans against the wall, watching, as if he is unsure what to do or how to act.

The Fate leans toward me, his gaze intent on my face. "Tell me what has happened."

"My uncle . . . Master Swan . . . has betrayed my father," I say, my voice sounding stuttered. I realize my hands are trembling. "Master Swan started a rebellion and now has my father in captivity." I look down at the scythe. "I would have never left with this if I had known my father would fall before Master Swan."

The silence in the house is disturbed only by the howling wind outside.

"I have crossed paths with Swan a time or two," the Fate said. "He must have a lot of support in the Underworld to gain power over your father."

"Yes," I exhale. I feel the prince's gaze on me although I am not looking at him. I can feel his pity as well.

"And Swan must be asking you to bring back the scythe," the Fate continues. "So that he can hold full power."

My answer is still quiet. "Yes." My eyes sting with tears. I have not cried much in my life, but it seems this would be the occasion to do so.

"You are mind-connected?" he asks.

I do not speak; my nod is sufficient.

"What will you do?" The Fate seems genuinely concerned.

I rise from the chair and turn away from the two pairs of eyes watching me. "I will have to fight Master Swan for the kingdom," I say at last. "I might be able to defeat him one-on-one, but not if he has a rebel army there to defend him. I will have to find a way to meet him alone."

"Swan will make sure he's never alone," the Fate says.

He is right. It's clear that Master Swan has been planning to overtake the Underworld, collecting a rebel army willing to follow him, and now he's holding my father captive. Not only will this disrupt the doings of the Underworld, it will affect the souls on earth that will be lost without a reaper to deliver them to the Judgment.

I feel defeated, and the fight has not even started.

Then the prince straightens from where he's been leaning against the wall. "Why don't you raise your own army?"

Eight

CORA SWUNG HER gaze around to meet Leo's. He knew that she must be surprised that he'd made a suggestion. He didn't understand all that she and Master Fate were talking about, but the answer seemed obvious. If the so-called Master Swan had a rebellion group to protect and defend himself, then why couldn't Cora put together her own group? After all, she was a royal princess—or queen now, it seemed.

It was strange to think that she'd been thrust into her role as queen just as Leo had nearly been thrust into his as king because of two warring brothers. They had a lot in common.

Her eyes seemed to change color in the glow of the firelight, and Leo found it fascinating. He knew he shouldn't allow himself to become mesmerized by the daughter of the Grim Reaper. Leo was still having trouble processing that this female, this being, in front of him was from a place not of earth. That the Grim Reaper was real, and she was standing in Master Fate's house.

Cora hesitated before she said, "I have no way to raise an army from here. And when I return to the Underworld, my uncle will be waiting for me."

Leo had plenty of questions. "Can you not communicate with someone you trust?" He almost said "down there," but he wasn't entirely sure where the Underworld was.

Cora stared at him, and Leo almost felt she could read into his soul. Could she see that he was afraid to get too close to her because when he touched her he couldn't slow the pounding of his heart? And he was sure that was a dangerous thing.

"The Underworld is not like earth where you can send letters with riders on horseback," she said. "Only immortals can pass through the portal, such as myself and Fate."

"Fate?" Leo said, looking over at Master Fate. Then, it was like he'd found the missing piece of a puzzle he'd been looking for. "You're..."

Master Fate's mouth curved into a smile. "I am immortal, sir. And I have been around a lot longer than the Grim Reaper's daughter." He looked at Cora. "No offense, Your Highness, but you are not quite correct in your statement."

She arched a brow.

"Mortals can, and have, passed through the portal,"

Master Fate said. "At a great cost, of course, but it is possible."

Leo's pulse pounded. He felt as if he were standing on the front lines of a battle, and every soldier in his thousand-man army was ready for him to take the first step. Once he did, they would all follow, swords raised, arrows flying, spears sailing.

Leo placed a hand at the hilt of his sword and bowed before the woman reaper. "I am at your service, Your Highness."

He could feel her staring at him again. When he straightened up, her lips had parted as if she were about to say something, but no words came. He could not look away, not now. He wanted her to know that he meant every word he said. For whatever reason, he'd never felt so strongly about fighting for a cause. Not even his own father's pursuit of the throne of Navarre had drawn this much determination from him.

"Do you care to know the cost first, dear prince?" Master Fate said.

"It will not change my mind," Leo said, keeping his gaze locked with Cora's. His heart was thumping so hard he was sure the immortals could probably hear it. What was he getting himself into? He could keep hiding out at the hunting lodge, or he could go live in his father's palace, or he could follow this young woman to another realm.

Cora's eyes flashed, then she broke their connected gaze. She looked at Master Fate and said, "How does it work, and what is the cost?"

Master Fate took a step closer so that they were in a sort of circle, standing before the hearth and its glittering fire. "Any mortal who trespasses into the immortal world will give up his life as it's known to him." He spoke in a low tone, and Leo strained to hear it above the storm outside. "He can never return to his family, for he will age quickly. Upon sight, his family would recoil and banish him."

"What about the Fountain of Youth?" Cora asked.

Leo stared at her. The Fountain of Youth was but a fable told around bonfires.

Master Fate released a low chuckle that sounded ominous. "You would face the sirens and risk your own life to let him drink from the fountain?"

"I am nearly twenty-one, and I shall have access," she said.

Master Fate shook his head. "You'll not have access if Swan gets ahold of the scythe."

Cora exhaled.

Nothing Master Fate said sounded encouraging.

Cora's gaze moved to Leo once again. "You may become an old man before your time." She stepped away from the circle, gripping the scythe in her hand. "I cannot ask that of anyone."

But Leo wasn't going to let her leave and disappear into the night. "You own my soul, already, do you not?"

She hesitated.

Leo wasn't sure if that was a good or bad sign.

"I made no such trade," she confessed.

"How is that possible?" Master Fate said. "It is the way of the Underworld. The saving of one life is always exchanged for the life of another."

Cora narrowed her eyes at Master Fate. "Do not tell me my duties. I know them well."

Master Fate looked far from convinced or chagrined as he folded his arms over his chest. "So you are saying that Prince Leo is a free soul?"

She seemed to straighten before she answered. "I am."

Leo was not going to be left out of this conversation. "I have made my decision."

Master Fate narrowed his eyes, focusing solely on Leo, as the fire crackled behind him. "Once you pass through the portal, you'll be in a different realm of time. Your mortal body will age rapidly. And even if the queen risks her own safety to get you a vial from the Fountain of Youth, it will only slow the progression of your aging and not reverse it." He lowered his voice, keeping it firm. "You will not be able to return to Navarre as you can now. You'll be viewed as a changeling, and your parents would have no alternative save to cast you out and disinherit you."

Leo didn't answer for a moment. So what if he returned and he looked to be thirty or forty in years? He'd be the same age as his father. He could meet his parents in secret and tell them what happened. Surely they'd believe him. His father would then understand once and for all that Leo didn't care to take the throne of Navarre. Though, ironically, he'd just committed to helping a stranger fight for her royal domain. And who was Leo to stand up against immortals in another realm?

But something burned inside of him, something

fierce that he'd never felt before, not even on the battlefields fighting for the kingdom of Navarre.

He spoke the truth when he said, "I have nothing keeping me here. I do not aspire to my father's throne, nor will I ever." He met Cora's gaze and held it.

Her green eyes had widened, yet he saw that she believed him . . . bold as his offer was.

"Well then," Master Fate said, cutting into the tension of the room. "I will come along too."

Cora snapped her head to look at Master Fate. "No," she said. "If Master Swan captures you, he will have even more power."

"I no longer serve at the Judgment Bar," Master Fate said.

"It doesn't matter," Cora said. "You still have the power to give eternal salvation or damnation. Master Swan won't stop with just ruling the Underworld."

Master Fate gave a slow, thoughtful nod. "You are right, Your Highness." And then he straightened and shuffled forward. "I might be an old man, and I might have once been the one to decide a soul's fate, but I will not sit in this hovel of a house on earth while a young immortal queen and a misguided mortal prince fight for what should be my cause too. I have but one weapon against Master Swan. Any contact with my amulet will kill him."

Leo looked to him, surprised at this revelation. It also made hope bloom and spread through him. With Master Fate at their side, they had a deadly weapon to use against Cora's uncle.

"If you are separated from your amulet, you will die," Cora said, her voice trembling. Leo watched her blink her eyes a couple of times and swallow against the emotion that had crept into her voice.

"I well know the risks, Your Highness," Master Fate said. "My life has served its purpose much longer than I've ever expected, my queen."

Cora remained quiet for a moment, and all the while Leo's heart pounded as he wondered what her response would be. Would she accept his offer?

When she finally spoke, she said, "I am not queen—not yet."

He knew how she felt, at least on one level. He'd been in his father's room when he'd been dying—had actually seen him die—then brought back to life. Cora didn't even have that opportunity with her father. Leo didn't know what battling against an immortal like Master Swan or whatever rebellion army he'd put together would be like, but he agreed with Master Fate. Leo believed in the cause. What happened in the Underworld would affect earth as well.

"You may not be crowned queen yet, Cora," Leo said. "But your father is in danger, and your uncle has no right to rule the Underworld while you are still in existence."

She exhaled slowly. "All right." She reached for Master Fate's hand and took it, then reached for Leo's. "We need a plan."

Nine

The prince has asked me to call him Leo, although it is strange to have a speaking relationship with a mortal. He calls the Fate by the title Master Fate, so I have adopted that as well.

We stand inside the crypt of an old monastery where Master Fate has led us.

"This will connect with the portal," Master Fate says, gesturing to the alcove beyond one of the stone caskets. He raises the candle he holds in his hand, and the glow casts moving shadows about the room.

I know there are multiple connections on earth that lead to the portal of the Underworld. I have come up through only one of them—when I was to fetch the new king of Navarre's soul.

Still, I gaze at the dark, cobwebbed alcove and doubt. Although I know my doubt is more like fear—fear of the unknown. We are standing in the small space of the crypt, so close-quartered that we can hear one another breathing.

I look over at Leo. His jaw is clenched tight, and he's withdrawn his own mortal sword, holding it securely at his side. By the breadth of his shoulders and the roped muscles in his forearms, I am sure that he's strong—for a mortal.

But will he be any sort of match against Master Swan or his army?

Next, I look at Master Fate. The Fate has existed a good number of decades, and he has aged significantly on earth. A vial from the Fountain of Youth might make him a stronger immortal. But it will not make him untouchable. If I cannot defeat Master Swan with the scythe, then Master Fate's amulet will have enough power to overcome my uncle.

The Fate's offer humbles me. I know that my father commands great loyalty, but I have not been crowned yet, and I cannot fully expect to step into my father's place so completely.

"Ready?" Master Fate asks.

Leo looks over at me, and our eyes connect. I am both comforted that he is by my side and filled with regret since I know that he is in the greatest danger out of the three of us. His mortal sword will only be the smallest of deterrents in a fight against immortals.

Leo holds my gaze, and I see the confidence in his blue eyes, and it makes my heart soar to a height that I have never before experienced. I realize then that he would be a formidable foe in any sort of battle.

If I but move one step toward him, our arms would touch.

"We must hold hands as we step into the alcove so that we aren't separated," Master Fate says.

I secure the scythe in the belt about my waist. This is not the first time I've grasped Leo's hands, but it feels more significant somehow. His fingers intertwine with mine. His hand is warm and solid and strong. My heart hitches, and I wonder at the way my pulse races all the way down to my toes. I can almost hear his heart beat, and his scent is stronger in this small space. The forest pine and deep spice that mortal men seem to exude is not lost on me.

Master Fate grasps my other hand. In contrast, his fingers are long, dry and cool. I feel that one of my hands is holding life, the other death.

We step forward together and move into the alcove that seems to hold centuries' worth of dust.

The stone and earth start to shift as soon as my feet touch the hard-packed dirt. Leo's grip tightens on mine, and I squeeze back. I know what to expect in the portal, and I anticipate the weightlessness that follows for several moments, but this will be a new experience for Leo.

I keep my eyes open so that I can watch him. Shades of gray swirl around us, tugging at my clothing and cloak, and the stone alcove simply melts away. We are in a void of no light, no darkness, no sound. Only gray everywhere.

When the gray softens and divides into the white of a hard marble floor and the velvet black of the walls of the hidden room behind the throne room of the Underworld, I hold my breath for a moment. Listening.

The throne room sounds empty.

I eventually become aware of the two standing beside me. Master Fate releases my hand first, and it's only then that I realize how hard I'd been gripping it. I relax the hand that is holding Leo's, and the loss of touch and sensation is immediate.

And then Master Fate pushes through the narrow corridor that leads to the throne room. I swallow and follow after him, with Leo right behind me.

I stop cold when I step out into the room. Next to me, Master Fate gapes at the site.

At least a dozen courtiers are lying on the floor, their bodies twisted in unnatural positions. They are clearly dead. Their robes are varied colors, so they are from different sectors of the Underworld. My gaze lands on a young man in a blue shirt and pants. Without turning him over, I know it is Rain, the young errand boy from the blue corridor. His smile will be forever gone now.

Leo steps past me, his hands on his hips as he surveys the damage. Tapestries have been torn from the walls as if by a wild beast. The large oval table has been severed in two, one half slightly larger than the other. Something drips, although I see no sign of water. There are no markings of the manner of death on the bodies that are strewn before us. But I know the cause.

The Grim Reaper has the power to stop a heart, and since he's imprisoned and I was above on earth, Master Swan used death magic on the courtiers. He stopped each of their hearts.

Leo drops to his knees next to the young boy Rain and picks up a lifeless limb. I realize that he's checking for a pulse.

I open my mouth to speak, but my voice catches.

"They are all dead, Prince," Master Fate says for me.

Leo lifts his head, and his blue, blue eyes are filled with grief. I am surprised to see him affected this way. "How were they killed?" he asks.

I don't know why it matters, but perhaps I do not completely understand mortals.

As Master Fate explains how a reaper has power over the hearts of immortals, I find that I too have sunk to my knees. I can't stop looking at the lifeless bodies. This is irony in itself. I, who am Mistress Grim and heir to the throne of the Underworld, have been brought to my knees by the sight of death.

Is it because they are my own kind? Or because I am not quite ready to shoulder the responsibilities of the kingdom?

When Leo finally stands after releasing Rain's arm, he circles the room, walking slowly. The questions in his gaze seep through me. How long has Master Swan been planning his defeat of my father? And how long do I have before he discovers I've returned?

I know it won't be long before Master Swan senses I am here. We are mind-connected, and even when I don't speak through channeling, he is perceptive. Still, I cannot move, and I keep my hands clenched together. The shock and grief have overwhelmed me. If Master Swan could kill so many immortals in one room, what of the rest of the kingdom? What of my father?

Master Fate speaks to Leo in a low voice, then begins to move the bodies, rearranging them into more dignified poses. He slides them together so that they are shoulder to shoulder, hip to hip. Leo helps him, and between the two of them, the work is soon finished.

Next they work on gathering the remnants of the tapestries and folding them together, and all the while I am kneeling, unable to move. Leo leaves the split table pieces where they have toppled. Master Fate begins a low chant, and I assume he is blessing their souls—although their souls have long since departed. Those of the Underworld do not need an escort to Judgment.

"Cora," Leo says in a whisper. He's reached my side, and his hand touches my shoulder.

Tears burn in my eyes at the concern he is showing for a realm he is not even connected to.

And then he kneels next to me.

It happens at the same time. I lean against him, and Leo wraps his arms about me. I have never been held by a mortal before; Leo is the first one I have ever touched. It is different than my father's embrace or a handshake greeting with a courtier.

"We will free your father and defeat your uncle," he says.

How can he know this? I want to believe his words.

Next to me, the scythe seems like a cold, cruel thing, but I will gladly wield it against the immortal who would tear apart the throne room—the very symbol of my father's decades of rule.

"Master Fate says that we must move quickly," Leo continues. "Your uncle will soon know we're here. We've done all we can here for now."

He is right. Master Fate is right.

Leo smooths back the tangled hair from my cheek, and I want to stay here, in his embrace, for much longer. I look up at him, and a new sense of urgency strikes me.

Leo has aged—it is a small change, but I notice it. His face has thinned, his hair is longer, and dark scruff has grown on his cheeks and chin where there was smooth skin before.

I reach up and touch his face. "We must hurry."

He nods but doesn't seem to want to move away from our connection any more than I do.

Finally, I drop my hand, and he releases me. Cool air seems to rush between us. He rises to his feet, then holds out his hand. I grasp it and allow him to pull me up.

Then I remove the scythe from my belt. I do not know what we'll find outside the throne room—more death? An army of rebels?

Master Fate waits for Leo and I to join him at the door, and I lift the heavy latch on the wall next to it. Then I shove the door open.

The corridor is absolutely silent, but I am not fooled.

Master Fate makes as if to lead the way, but I step ahead of him and stride down the corridor. The smell of the place is off. The dirt-and-rock smell I am accustomed to is different.

Now I smell rot.

I slow as I near the end of the corridor. Just beyond is the commons. I can hear the Fountain of Youth gurgling away, and this gives me hope. Feeling more confident, I step out of the corridor.

We are not alone. This is the first feeling that washes

over me. The other feeling is one of dismay. For the Fountain of Youth is no longer guarded by the three sirens. And the crystal blue water does not cascade up and over the fountain and tumble into the carved stone pool.

The water is a muddy brown, and it looks nothing like the elixir of youth.

Panic shoots through me—if the fountain has been tainted then the properties of eternal youth are already tainted.

A movement across the commons confirms my first impression. We are not alone. I cannot tell who or what moved—all I know is that whatever creature it is, it's now disappeared into the red corridor, where my father used to live.

Does this mean that Master Swan has now taken over even the red corridor?

"The fountain," Master Fate whispers, directing my attention back to it.

It's bubbling as if it's sitting over a hot fire. And the smell of rot is growing stronger. I feel compelled to walk to the fountain, and Master Fate doesn't protest. He only follows with Leo close behind.

My stomach clenches tight as I approach. I think I know even before I see it.

The once-honey-colored hair of the siren women is now dark because of the muddied water. They have been dead for at least a day, their lithe bodies now bloated beneath the colored water. It's then I realize the color of the water isn't brown, but a rusty red—the color of the sirens' blood.

If there is one thing that the water from the Fountain of Youth must never come in contact with, it's blood. It's a sure contaminant.

I turn to Leo, and I know it's not my imagination that his shoulders have broadened into the size of a full man's. He now has a short beard. His gaze meets mine, and his eyes flash with anger . . . and knowledge. Without saying anything, he knows that his age can now never be slowed or reversed.

Instead of turning and fleeing back to the throne room where he could reenter the portal and return to earth as a man in his late twenties, he steps toward me.

He grasps my free hand, lifts it to his mouth, and presses a kiss on the top.

Master Fate says nothing, although I can feel the burn of revenge reaching out from him to me.

The courtiers are dead. The sirens are dead.

The Underworld is like a beast silently breathing, ready to pounce.

Leo releases my hand, and a sound behind me makes his gaze shift. His eyes widen at whatever he is seeing.

The skin along the back of my neck and shoulders prickles, and I turn. There, at the entryways to each of the corridors, stand creatures that I hoped I would never have to face. Or fight.

Ten

"Reapers," Master Fate whispered, and Leo felt a shiver run through his body. He sensed that these reapers were not logical or "good" immortals like Cora and her father. "Swan has turned the reapers," Master Fate continued. "No wonder he thinks he can become the next king of the Underworld. If he can command the reapers, he can command life and death."

Leo wanted to ask more questions about how they could defeat these reapers and get to their real target—Swan. The reapers seemed to be multiplying, and their dark cloaks were mostly in hues of black and deep brown; they were beings that would be indistinguishable in dark alleys. There were male and female, their skin pale, their eyes large and luminous.

If Leo didn't know who the reapers were and what they did, he might think them beautiful. Like Cora. Yet none of the female reapers were as captivating to Leo as Cora.

Each of the reapers had short scythes, similar to

Cora's, although different too. The gleaming metal reminded Leo of the battles of Navarre as the two sides charged each other, swords and spears ready.

But these reapers weren't charging. They were moving as a whole, surrounding Leo and his two companions, sorely outnumbering the three of them.

Leo was impressed that Cora didn't step back or seem to look for cover. She held her scythe out in front of her and was staring at the corridor that was painted red as if she were waiting for someone else to appear.

In fact, she was practically ignoring the approaching mass of reapers. Master Fate was whispering again, and Leo had to focus above the loud thump of his heart to hear the words.

"The reapers cannot touch Mistress Grim since her power outweighs theirs," Master Fate said. "Swan knows this, but he is using the reapers against us."

Leo inhaled, then let out his breath in a slow hiss. He had no problem fighting off the reapers, but he wondered how long he'd last against the several dozen that had now gathered. He estimated over sixty in number now.

"How do we hold them off?" Leo asked.

"You are but a small deterrent. Your mortal sword can only wound, not kill. So they will try to get to me first," Master Fate continued. "With my death, the amulet has no use unless they have a Fate on their side. By killing me, they will make Swan more invincible."

And Cora would have the only weapon against her uncle.

"What do you want me to do, Cora?" Leo asked.

"Don't let them touch Master Fate," she said, her tone hard. She didn't move her gaze from the entrance of the red corridor.

A low hum had started to fill the room, and Leo realized the reapers were making the sound. It was both beautiful and awful at the same time and reminded Leo of a disjointed religious incantation.

He tried to make eye contact with the reapers that were closing in, but they seemed to be either looking at Cora or Master Fate. Leo kept his sword in his right hand and then removed a smaller dagger strapped to his calf. He gripped the dagger with his left hand, ready for anything.

Leo turned, keeping his back to Cora, waiting for the first attack. She started walking toward the fountain then, and Leo stepped backward, keeping his body between her and the advancing reapers. She stepped up on the stone ledge of the pool, and this seemed to incite the other immortals.

The musical hum morphed into more of a guttural scream, and suddenly two of the reapers lunged at Leo. His heart dropped as his pulse spiked at the same time.

The battle had begun.

Leo swung his sword, surprised at the weightlessness of it. He knew that his body had aged because of the way that Cora had looked at him earlier. But he hadn't thought that it would be to his advantage. Now he seemed to have the strength and skill of a man in his late twenties, versus a young man who'd only fought in a handful of battles.

The male reaper was fast, though, and moved out of the way just before Leo's sword connected with the reaper's torso. Leo spun on his feet and lunged again, this time striking his target.

The reaper's cry sailed above the rest of the sounds reverberating throughout the room. He crumpled to the ground and stopped moving. There was no blood, no sign of a gash, but the reaper was obviously seriously injured. Whether or not he was dead was another matter.

But Leo didn't have time to triumph because a female reaper was already swinging her scythe at his head. Leo ducked and slashed at her ankles. Again his sword made contact. The female howled and toppled over.

Another reaper was upon him before Leo could check how Master Fate or Cora were faring. The reapers seemed to be coming at him two at a time now. Leo kept swinging, slashing into reaper after reaper as their luminous eyes stared at him and their screeches filled the air.

Leo estimated he'd defeated about fifteen of the immortals when something shoved him from behind. Leo whirled to find Master Fate collapsed on the ground, his skin pale. Two reapers leapt atop of the Fate, and Leo stabbed both of the reapers in their necks. Then he rolled the immortals off Master Fate, hoping that he was not beyond saving.

But Leo didn't have time to even assess Master Fate's condition because another surge of reapers had arrived. Dodging and striking, Leo took down four more reapers. His muscles burned, and his body was soaked in perspiration, but he felt strong as adrenaline surged through his body.

Cora was still standing upon the stone wall where she battled any reaper who tried to reach her. Her scythe made quick work of her attackers.

Leo continued to fight, losing count of how many reapers he sent to the floor and losing track of any sense of time. All he knew was that the reapers kept coming, and coming. Master Fate was not getting up either, and Cora continued to hold back any of the reapers that approached her.

Somehow Leo kept going despite the fact that it seemed he was the only one in the battle against the reapers. He hadn't thought to ask how many reapers could possibly be inhabiting the Underworld, but he knew that at some point his strength would give out.

"Leo," Cora said above him, but he barely registered the sound over the cries of the immortals.

And then, just as if someone blew out a candle flame, the reapers all paused, then stepped backward, moving into the corridors they'd poured out of only moments before.

Their gazes were focused at a place beyond Leo. He turned to see where they were looking. Cora had moved off the stone wall and was advancing toward the red corridor. There in the entry stood a thin immortal, not much taller than Cora. His hair was nearly white, but not because he was an old man. His pale skin reminded Leo of an albino person.

He was no doubt Master Swan. His robe was a deep scarlet, and it looked as if it was stained with something dark. The expression on his face made Leo's stomach twist. Swan looked as if he were enjoying every moment of the battle.

Leo started to follow Cora. Master Fate was still on the ground, but looked to be breathing. Leo didn't know Cora's intentions, but he wasn't about to let her face Swan alone. And now that the reapers had withdrawn, Leo had a chance to catch his breath.

Cora wasn't stopping, so Leo hurried to catch up with her impossibly brisk stride. Was she just going to take a swing at Swan with her scythe?

Swan's left arm was hanging at his side, but Leo didn't miss the fact that he had his own scythe in the other hand.

The courtyard held an eerie stillness to it, and virtually the only sound was Cora's footsteps.

Master Swan released a low chuckle, and that's when Cora's step seemed to falter. "I knew you would return," the man's inky voice filled the silence.

Cora didn't hesitate. She lunged straight for Master Swan, both hands gripping the scythe held out in front of her.

Eleven

THE MOMENT I see Master Swan's amber eyes and pale face, all anticipation and fear flee my body. I can only think of one thing. To destroy my uncle. He has brought disorder and chaos to the Underworld, so much so that even the reapers have congregated down here, which means that souls have been left trapped in dying bodies on earth.

I stride toward him, too furious to care about my well-being. Master Fate has been injured, and Leo won't last much longer. I alone need to defeat Swan now. Only one of us can remain in the Underworld.

When he laughs at me, something inside boils over, and I lunge for him, hoping that I can end his existence once and for all. I hear Leo calling to me, but it is too late. I have already made contact.

Swan twists out of the way, and his thin but strong hand grasps the handle of the scythe. I have been trained by him for years, yet his strength surprises me. I refuse to let him wrest the scythe away from me. It will take my death to pry the scythe from my determined fingers.

Swan tugs the scythe toward him, and I come with it. Then I see his intentions. He raises his own scythe and swings it wide. It will not kill me, but it might be enough to injure me and give him the advantage.

But before the weapon connects with my torso, something deflects it.

Leo's sword.

It's my turn to twist away now, and I use Leo's element of surprise to tear the scythe from Swan's hold. The action causes me to lose my balance, and I crash to the hard floor. Swan and Leo begin to circle each other, each of them looking like they would welcome death.

Panic races through me. I have never been defended in such a manner, and never, of course, by a mortal. The outcome can't be good.

I scoot back until I reach the wall of the corridor. The entire palace seems to be holding its breath as immortal and mortal face off.

I watch the two fight while my thoughts tumble as I try to think of how to save Leo and defeat Swan. Leo's arms are roped with defined muscles. His beard has grown below his chin, and his face is more square and more thin. I guess him to be at least thirty years of age now, and his abilities have only seemed to expand. He is no longer a young man but has the look of a seasoned warrior.

The smile on Swan's face seems to dim as he realizes the same thing I do. Still, Leo is mortal. Swan immortal.

Leo makes the first move, breaking their circle. He brings his sword down upon the scythe, and I hear a crack.

My heart soars. Leo is not only strong and fierce, but he is wise. His blow has compromised the strength of my uncle's weapon. My uncle is no fool, though. The weapon is still of use, and he hurls it with all his might straight at Leo's head.

I scream.

Leo dodges the blade, and it misses a fatal blow. But the scythe has clipped his shoulder, and blood runs red down his arm. Then it's as if time slows, and I see Swan's scythe arc above me.

I scramble out of the way, twisting my ankle as I move. The pain is sharp and fierce. I'm off-balance and fall to one knee, nearly losing my grip on my own scythe.

Swan sees that I've fallen, and instead of turning on me, he once again lashes out at Leo.

The prince is quicker than I could have ever imagined—almost immortally fast—and he drives his sword against Swan's legs. Swan is struck, but a mortal sword would never be fatal to an immortal.

I hope it's enough to gain the upper hand, though. As I struggle to my feet, Swan grasps for the wall to hold himself upright. His eyes are full of pain, but the hardness remains.

I cannot think that this is the man who's been my tutor for nearly seven years. That my father trusted. Who I trusted. But he has committed the ultimate betrayal, and in the Underworld there is only room for one king.

Until my father departs his immortal existence, I will fight on his behalf.

I lunge toward Swan and bring my scythe down against his neck. But I have misjudged his weakness. He is waiting for me, and just before I connect the blade against his neck, he drives his foot against my stomach.

The breath is knocked out of me, and I am once again forced to my knees. The impact loosens my grip on the scythe, and Master Swan is ready. He wrenches it upward, his hands covering mine, and brings it down upon my own head.

I wait for the blow, knowing that I've failed so many, including Prince Leo, the Fate, and all the reapers who will eventually realize what they've traded to follow after Swan. But instead of the scythe knocking me the rest of the way to the ground, Leo's shoulder makes contact with my side, and the scythe hits him instead.

My breath whooshes out of me. Leo has collapsed on top of me. His warm and heavy weight seems to cover me like a blanket, yet horror washes through me as I guess that he is dead.

But something has happened to Master Swan. He is lying on the ground, merely an arm's length away. I see him out of the corner of my eye because I cannot turn my head. The weight of Leo's shoulder is pressing against my throat.

What's happened to Swan? Why is he lying on the ground as if I'd succeeded with the scythe? And then I see another body lying beyond Swan.

The Fate has somehow risen from his earlier injury and has done something to Swan.

I wriggle beneath Leo and, with all my strength, I push him off, then lean up on an elbow to look over at Master Fate.

"No," I whisper to myself. The amulet about his neck is cracked right down the middle. It no longer glows but looks like a dark indigo stain on the Fate's tunic.

I roll to my side and push up to my knees. I crawl the few feet over to the Fate's body. The skin about his mouth and nose are blue. It's as if he's been suffocated in a room full of air. My heart wrenches. He is dead. This Fate has given his life in order to save mine.

Next, my gaze moves to Master Swan.

The man was thin and wiry during his immortality, but death makes him look skeletal. Two deceased immortals lie on the floor in front of me, and I cannot do it . . . I cannot take their souls.

I can feel their souls reaching out to me, begging me to take them to their Judgments. I should feel vengeful and want to lead Master Swan to his eternal damnation. But I don't want to serve him in any way.

I must see if Leo is beyond help.

With trembling hands, I make my way to where he is lying facedown. I touch his hair and feel warmth. I can only hope that it is a good sign. From the edges of my vision, I catch a glimpse of the reapers—they've returned. They are silent now, no longer screaming their battle cries.

Some of them start to tend to those who've fallen. Others approach me, but I don't pay them any heed.

"Leo?" I whisper, close to his ear. Blood has dried upon his skin, and I run my fingers over the dried substance. I have never touched blood before. "Wake up, Leo," I say again.

I am denying the fact that his soul is trying to escape his body. It's trying to free itself, to move on. I need to get him to a mortal physician. I turn Leo to his side. The blood extends along the edge of his tunic and along his sleeve. Everywhere. There is too much blood.

His eyes are closed, and his breathing faint.

"Leo," I say, my voice coming out in a sob. "Wake up." I turn to look for a reaper to help me. Their eyes are dark, empty, and I know it will be a while before I can command them. The power that Master Swan had over them will take time to wear off.

With Master Fate gone, I need to get Leo to the portal by myself. I need to get him to earth so that he can be healed. Once he leaves the Underworld, his aging process will slow again.

I reach around him, and with both hands I turn him over onto his back. He is heavier than I thought.

"Come on, Leo," I say, gazing at his closed eyelids. His jaw is more defined, stronger, and his cheeks more hollow, making his cheekbones more prominent. I feel the reapers watching me, although none of them step forward to help. So I rise and hook my arms behind his shoulders and start dragging him toward the throne room.

My muscles protest, but I grit my teeth and continue to drag him bit by bit.

As I approach the Fountain of Youth, I stare at the change. The murky, stained water has cleared. It's as if there had been no destruction or death in the fountain. I set Leo down and hurry over. The bodies of the sirens are gone, and in their place is clear blue water. I do not know if the fountain still has the healing properties that it once did or if it's perhaps now a different kind of poison. But I can't pass up this chance.

I scoop the water in my hand, finding it cool, and I hurry to Leo's side and dribble it into his mouth.

"Drink, Leo," I say. His lips don't move, and I hope that something has passed through his mouth and into his throat.

Again, I hurry to the fountain, scoop another handful, and pour it over Leo's mouth. He doesn't swallow or open his eyes. I may be too late. I lift his shoulders again and start to drag him.

And that's when the first rumble starts.

My heart is already racing in panic, and I don't know how much more it can keep beating. The very ground is shifting beneath my feet.

It's stronger than the tremor that foretold the king of Navarre's death. But as the water in the Fountain of Youth sloshes over the side of the stone wall, I know that this tremor is more than just a warning.

It sounds as if the very jaws of the Underworld have opened with displeasure.

The reapers are starting to panic too, and their screeching cries start up again. I wish I had the strength of my father, or even the help of Master Fate. I try to move faster, pulling Leo with me, but my strength is quickly depleting as I half drag him toward the throne room.

The ground sways, and I hear a crashing sound behind me. Turning, I see the balustrade above the entry to the throne room crumble to the floor.

"No," I cry out. It seems to be the only word in my vocabulary. If the entryway collapses, I'll lose access to the portal. Leo will die.

I'm crying, sobbing, yet I continue to move as dust and bits of stone choke the air. My heart is ready to burst, my lungs are burning, and my arms and legs feel as if they are made of nothing, when suddenly, the weight of Leo lifts.

I look up. A tall figure in a torn, black cloak is picking up Leo.

I stare for several heartbeats before I find my voice. "Father!"

Twelve

I CANNOT BELIEVE what I am seeing. My father is carrying Leo in his arms and striding into the throne room. I follow, scurrying after him as emotions war within me. I have so many questions. But first, I am filled with relief.

My father is alive.

And he is taking Leo to safety.

But there is no more time. The ground shudders violently, and I am almost thrown to the floor. I manage to keep my balance as the very stones that make up the walls shift, and I follow my father behind the torn tapestry.

Once inside, I grasp his arm so that we might arrive at the same location on earth. Just before we are swept into the vortex, my father says, "Thank you, Cora."

I close my eyes against the gray and just let everything inside of me go numb. The events of the last day have been nothing like I'd ever thought to experience. My father is alive, though, and that's all that matters in the end. If Leo lives, I will be even happier and will feel that the Fate's death has been fully avenged.

My father will know what to do about the rebellious reapers. He'll know what to do about the trapped souls on earth. He'll know what to do about the crumbling Underworld we've just left. And I can only hope he'll know how to find a physician.

The moments pass, and when the air grows still and moist, I know we've arrived on the other side of the portal.

I open my eyes to see that it's morning, and the early sun glints off a dew-laden meadow.

I look about quickly, noting that we are not near a town or village. How does my father plan to get help for Leo?

I should have known better than to doubt him, for before I can speak, my father sets Leo down, then brings two fingers to his lips and whistles.

The whistle is low, like a hum, but I know that many creatures on the earth can hear it.

I hear the beast before I see him. The earth seems to tremble at the sound as well. It isn't long before I see the massive stallion. Although my father has told me of Grande, I have never met him. Many reapers have horses, or stallions, upon the earth. These stallions are not earthly beasts, though. They exist only to serve their master—whichever reaper that happens to be.

Grande approaches, his eyes a dark gray, his coat and mane nearly black. He looks like the clouds of a spring storm. The beast's eyes shift to me with wariness as he comes to a halt before his master.

"Grande," my father says. "This is my daughter, Cora."

The horse nods its head and seems to understand, for its prancing hooves go still.

"You will transport the prince to the healer in the next village," my father says as he strokes the horse's forehead.

I am certain the beast understands.

Then my father picks up Leo and settles him onto the back of the horse.

Leo lies like he is a sleeping child, but he is breathing, so I take hope in that. He has not aged further since he collapsed and I dribbled the Fountain of Youth water on him. Is this because his aging has slowed or because he is dying?

"Will you not guide the horse?" I ask after my father gives Grande more instructions. "Leo will fall off with no one to hold him in place."

"Grande will take care of him," my father says, then pats the horse on the side.

The horse starts to move forward, and before I can ask more questions, Grande is already crossing the meadow.

"Do you think he'll live?" I ask my father. Now that we are on earth, and now that Leo is back among his own kind, all the events over the past day are starting to collide in my mind.

"I don't know, Cora," my father says. He grasps my arms. "Are you all right? I didn't know what to expect when the prison bars shook out of their stone molds. All I knew was that Swan was dead."

"I'm all right," I say, and then I start to cry. I had been all right—at least able to school my emotions—until he had to *ask* me if I was all right.

My father's arms wrap around me, and I lean into his solid strength. If anyone happened to come upon us in this meadow, I knew we would be a strange sight to behold. The Grim Reaper comforting his crying daughter.

So much has been lost, and so much needs to be done.

"The reapers," I say against his chest, my thoughts spinning. I draw away from him and look up. "They've left souls in dead bodies. I could smell it before I came through the portal with the Fate and the prince."

"We need to return and restore order," my father says, dropping his arms. "And eventually I want to know how you came to bring a mortal into the Underworld. It seems he possesses the sight, but that is not enough to establish contact with him. All mortals, no matter their talents, are better off on earth." His voice is firm, with implied warning, but for now that conversation will have to wait.

And I will wonder later how many rules I have broken.

"Come," my father says, motioning with his hand. "The sooner we return, the sooner the order can be re-stored."

I hesitate, and I know I am wrong for it, but my heart is already taking control. "I must see how he fares," I say.

My father's dark brows tug together, and he studies

me. "Although we are immortal, we still experience very mortal emotions. As the queen of the Underworld, you must understand all that entails and the need to rise above the emotions that interfere with your reign."

He is right. But my stomach is twisting, and my pulse is pounding. I know that my father will never demand that I return to the Underworld with him. I may be his daughter, but I am also royalty.

"I will come soon," I say.

His eyes remain steady on me. "Do you understand that I cannot unite the reapers? It needs to be done by you or they will not see you as their leader. If I do it, you'll lose respect. There will be another risk for a rebellion, and you know what the last one cost . . . and is still costing."

A Fate has died. The next heir after me has been killed. The prince of Navarre is at death's door. Souls all across the world are trapped inside decaying bodies.

Still, I step away from my father.

His eyes shift. He knows that I've made up my mind, and he isn't happy about it.

"Cora, you will regret this."

My breathing is faint. If I leave the prince here, to *his* fate, and he dies, I will also regret not checking on him. Just to see if he'll live. That is all I intend.

"Father, I can't explain now, but I must go," I tell him. "I will return soon."

He's listening, but he isn't pleased with my decision.

Before he can respond or dissuade me, I turn from him and hurry across the meadow. I follow the path Grande has made through the dew-spotted land.

I know my father is watching me, but he doesn't call

out. He doesn't order me back, which he has the power to do. I am never more relieved than at this moment, because he chooses to let me choose.

I pick up my pace and reach a path that follows a thin line of trees. Eventually it opens up onto a narrow road, and in the distance, beyond a set of hills, I see smoke rising from a small collection of houses. This is not a village or a town but only a hamlet.

I hope there is a trained physician in the region and that Leo is with him now.

I am running, and hoping, and feeling helpless at the same time. There is no sign of Grande.

As the road climbs over the hill, the sun crests over the eastern horizon. If I had but time to stop and appreciate the sights of the earth, the peaceful setting might have been a balm. But I cannot slow my pace because my greatest fear is that I will be too late.

Then the scent comes in on the morning breeze—the smell of rot—and I know that the reapers have neglected even this tiny hamlet as well. I just hope, with everything that I've ever hoped, that the dead doesn't include the prince.

Once I reach the first farmhouse, I allow myself to slow. But there is no sign of Grande at the first house.

So I continue, looking from thatched-roof house to what look like no more than hovels. Smoke from indoor hearths billows from several of the homes, and for a few moments, the scent of cooking overpowers the rotting.

The main square is quiet. A couple of dogs, who were sleeping next to a well, lift their heads as I approach. One of them jumps to his feet and lets out a rapid succession of barks. The second dog only whines and sprints away as if I were chasing it. The barking dog eventually follows the first dog, and I am glad to be rid of them.

I do not need the villagers to come out of their homes and wonder at the barking dogs. I've heard more than one reaper's story about being seen by mortals who have the sight and then being hunted as if they were witches. And the mortals with the sight usually fare no better. No one wins when a reaper is cornered.

But I cannot wait until night falls to finish this trek. Not only is my father waiting for me, but I must see how Leo fares. I continue past the main square and make my way to another cluster of thatched-roof houses.

And then I slow. Grande is standing next to a place that looks more like a hovel. It's built into a hillside, and the door is wide open. I do not know what to expect, but I hurry forward.

Grande turns his head as I near and blinks his dark gray eyes as if to say, "What took you so long?"

I merely nod and stop just outside the entrance.

Inside, the dimness makes it hard to focus at first. But there is a fire in the hearth and a few candles burning, casting haphazard shadows against the bare floor and bare walls.

Two chairs are positioned near the hearth, and a young child sits in one of them, her knees pulled up to her chest. A blanket has been tucked around her small frame, and she sucks on two fingers. She looks at me with curiosity but says nothing. For a strange moment, I wonder if the child is mute. I do know with certainty she can see me, for she is looking straight at me.

And then I hear a rasp of words from beyond the main room, coming from somewhere deep inside the hovel.

I decide not to question the child, who in fact may be too young to talk, and I step across the threshold.

The scent of the room is a mixture of pine and sage—much better than the rotting smell that moves on the breeze outside.

I follow the deep voice along a narrow corridor lined with low tables. The hovel goes back into the hillside, and the damp surrounds me as I pass the tables filled with herbs and other dried plants and roots. The musty smell grows more dank as I move farther into the corridor.

And then the voice stops, and ahead of me a door creaks open.

A woman stands there, and although she seems tiny with a hunched back, her eyes are bright and watchful. The wrinkles on her face are like trails surrounding her mouth and eyes.

"I thought he was mad," she says in that low, raspy voice.

I realize that the voice I thought belonged to an old man belongs to this ancient woman. And the woman can see me. She must have the gift of sight.

"Is Prince Leo here?" I ask, knowing that I must sound anxious.

The woman smiles, her gapped teeth making her look strangely youthful. "Yes, the prince is 'ere." And then she bends into a deep bow. "O Queen."

"I—I am not yet queen," I say. "And I am here to inquire about the prince's health. Is he . . ."

The woman is still smiling at me, even after she rises from her bow. "He's alive, if that's what ye are so interested in knowing." Her laughter is abrupt, rude even, but it doesn't bother me in the least.

For her words are like the most beautiful song ever sung. The prince is alive.

"How—how is he?" I stumble again over my words because all my thoughts have collided.

The woman shifts to one side of the door opening and lifts a gnarled hand. "Come and see for yerself."

She shuffles aside some more, and I realize that she means for me to pass by her and enter the room.

There is no light in the room, and I wonder what I will find. I would have walked through a field of fire if it meant seeing how Leo was doing.

My first impression of the room is that it smells of lavender and orange—an interesting and pungent combination.

No fire burns, but the room is pleasantly warm for being built so far into the hillside. Candles line a table that stands along the wall. Steam rises from a black kettle in the corner of the sparse room, and I decide that's where the scent is coming from.

Upon a long cushion on the floor a body is stretched out.

Without noticing any details, I know instinctively it is the prince.

He seems to be sleeping, for his breathing is deep and steady. His hair is a mixture of gold and amber in the candlelight.

I am by his side in an instant, dropping to my knees

so that I can get a close look at him. His eyes are closed, and his eyelashes look like smudges against his cheeks. A significant bruise travels along the left side of his jaw.

Then I notice that his tunic has been removed, and he's been covered with a length of cloth. His shoulders are bare, and two gashes have been neatly cleaned and stitched, although the surrounding skin is an angry red.

Next, my gaze moves to his throat and upper chest that are left uncovered. The pulse in his neck beats steady, and I become mesmerized by the rise and fall of his chest.

He is truly alive. Sleeping, but alive.

I don't mean to touch him, but I reach out a hand anyway and run my fingers along his arm and over his wrist, then along his fingers.

"Leo?" I whisper, not expecting him to respond.

But then his eyes flutter open.

Thirteen

Leo felt both cold and hot at the same time, as if he were swimming in a sun-warmed pond. The murky depths made his feet cold, but the sun on top of the water kept his shoulders and chest warm. Yet he did know that wherever he was, he wasn't in the water. The air about him was dry enough, and he was definitely not swimming.

He wasn't sure if he was awake or asleep or if he was in his father's palace or at the hunting lodge. He supposed he'd worry about it when he woke up. For now, he was content to continue drifting in and out of awareness. It was relaxing somehow to be half-awake and not fully understanding which day it was and what tasks lay ahead.

"Leo," a woman's voice said, cutting through the haze that had captured his mind.

That's when the pain started.

His body released whatever numbness it had been

holding on to, and Leo knew, without a doubt, he'd been in a battle. But which battle? His father had already won the kingdom of Navarre. His father sat securely on his throne . . . His father had almost died. No, he *had* died.

And then . . . he'd come back to life.

Leo's memories rushed through his mind, colliding into one another. The young woman in the cloak. Her eyes the color of summer green. Her hair golden-bronze. Her . . . scythe.

"Leo," the woman said again.

And then, like a fire blasting from a kiln, all Leo's memories hit him at once. He opened his eyes, and there she was, bent over him, watching.

Leo tried to speak, but his lips wouldn't cooperate, and he couldn't push any words out.

Cora smiled, and Leo realized he'd never seen her smile before. It made his heart feel like it was being squeezed. Her hair tumbled over her shoulders and hung down so that it brushed against his bare arms.

"You're alive," Cora said, brushing her fingers against his cheeks. Her caress told him he had a significant bruise on his jaw, and it hurt his skin to be touched, but whatever pain it caused didn't matter.

He'd gone into the Underworld and fought against a legion of reapers. He'd battled against Master Swan, and he'd watched Master Fate die . . . but then he remembered nothing after that. Was he still in the Underworld now?

Leo's stomach clenched. He must be an old man now. His skin would be wrinkled and spotted and his arms thin and weak. He wondered if he still had all his teeth and whether his hair had gone white or gray.

Cora moved closer and whispered, "I thought you'd died, my prince."

Was 'my prince' an endearment? For he knew that no earthly prince could ever rule over an immortal queen.

She was a queen, Leo realized, not for the first time. Here he was, wounded from battle, yet the queen of the Underworld had taken time to check on him.

He looked past her seeking eyes to scan the small room. The earthy scent was strong, mixed with lavender and something else. Light and shadows flickered on the ceiling above, telling Leo that there were candles burning somewhere out of his line of vision.

Had she found her father? Was he alive?

"How . . ." he managed to say. "How is your father?"

Cora blinked rapidly, then said, "He's safe. He helped me bring you here."

Leo gave a slow nod but then stopped when even his neck hurt.

Cora continued, "My father carried you to the portal and brought you to earth. I—I poured some water from the Fountain of Youth on you."

Leo tried to smile, but he only managed to inhale. "Did it work?" He meant it as a quip, but she was studying his face.

"The light isn't very good in here," she said. "But if it did work, it can take some time to be visible."

"How long have I been here?" Leo asked.

Another voice replied, and a hunched over woman stepped into view. "Only a few hours, Your Highness," she croaked. "Your youth and determination to live made my job easy."

Leo blinked and stared at the woman. "Are you a healer?" She was perhaps the oldest woman he'd ever seen. He couldn't begin to count the wrinkles on her face, and her body seemed to have shriveled up. Despite her appearance, her eyes were every bit as alert as a much younger woman's.

One side of her mouth lifted as if she found his question amusing. He'd also asked that same question of Cora when they first met.

"Some might call me a healer," the woman said. "I do not give myself any title, though; it's easier that way." She looked at Cora, then back to him. "You were so full of conversation when you arrived—at first I thought you were delirious to tell me that you'd met Mistress Grim and had been in a battle in the Underworld. But I see now that you were not delirious."

She placed a cold, gnarled hand on his bare shoulder. "You owe Mistress Grim your life. A debt to an immortal is a heavy burden. I can only hope you are up to the task."

Leo's gaze shifted to Cora. "I know," he said in a quiet voice. "I owe a lot more than my own life."

A small sound reached Leo's ears, and he couldn't tell if it was a crying child or a cat.

"I will return shortly," the woman said. "You will need to rest for several days until the good blood in your body can rid itself of any bad blood." The woman lifted her cold hand from his shoulder and shuffled away.

Soon the sound of the crying child stopped.

Before Cora could leave too, Leo had questions. "What happens now? Swan is dead, right? Does this mean you can now take your throne?" He was surprised when

Cora looked away. "Cora?'" he asked, although he knew it was a very informal way to address her.

"The battle isn't completely over," she said after a moment. "My father is waiting for me to return with him. I have to establish myself as a leader. We have to restore the order of reapers—in their rebellion, they've neglected hundreds of souls, probably thousands by now."

"So, why are you here?" Leo asked.

When her gaze met his, his heart gave a jolt. It was not logical to think that she cared about him—in a way that was impossible to consider—but he'd seen it in her eyes. If only for a brief moment.

His heart thudded, and then he pushed back the heat rising in his chest. He'd risked his life for her, and she was just returning the gratitude. Perhaps they were even, now that he'd helped her after she'd returned his father to life.

"I needed to know you were all right," she said in a stilted voice as if she wasn't sure what she should say or not say. "I needed to make sure you were alive."

Leo pushed up on his elbows so that he could start to clear his head, but the pain that shot through his body made him gasp.

"Don't move yet," Cora said. "The physician says it will be several days before you can get up."

Leo exhaled. He hated that he couldn't help her more and was instead lying helpless on a mat in someone's hut.

Despite the sharp pain every time he inhaled or exhaled, he said, "I need to sit up. Can you help me?"

She hesitated, then grasped his hand. He used her as an anchor to sit up on the pallet.

The blanket that had covered him to his chest slipped

to his waist. Her eyes followed the movement, then her gaze snapped back to his.

He wanted to smile at the soft red that bloomed on her cheeks.

Keeping a hold of her hand, he squeezed her fingers lightly. He'd touched her before, more than once, but she seemed to welcome his touch this time. "Because of you, my father is alive," he said. "And because of you again, I'm alive. You have been generous to my family. I don't know how to thank you, but I will do whatever I can to repay my debt. But now you must leave this place and help your father restore order."

"You're right," she said, but she didn't make any moves to leave. She didn't release his hand, and she didn't look away. They were sitting so that their faces were only a couple of handspans apart. "But I'm finding it difficult to leave because I won't know how you are faring when I'm gone."

Leo shook his head slowly. "My well-being is nothing compared to what you are facing. You don't need to worry about me. I'm already sitting up." He smiled, hoping she'd smile back.

She only continued to stare at him as if her thoughts were far away and she wasn't listening to a word he was saying.

"Your kingdom needs you, Cora," he continued. He had seen the chaos and confusion of the Underworld. The dead bodies. The spoiled Fountain of Youth. The rebellious reapers. She needed to return with her father to set things right.

But she was leaning closer, and his heart was thumping so hard he was sure she could hear it.

"Cora," he tried again, although the word came out only as a whisper. "You should go. Your father is waiting."

"Kiss me," she said, her face only a breath away now. Her eyes slid shut, and Leo couldn't keep his gaze from the dusky pink of her mouth.

He swallowed. "Is that a command, O Queen?"

Now she smiled, but she kept her eyes closed. "It is a command, and even though you're a mortal, you must follow my commands."

He wondered briefly if she'd ever kissed a mortal before, but then he decided it didn't matter. She was so close that Leo barely had to move to press his mouth against hers. Her lips were warm, soft, and welcoming.

He lifted his other hand to slide it behind her neck as he angled his mouth over hers to deepen the kiss. She tasted of honey and flowers and dark secrets and soft silk. She pressed against him as she kissed him back, her lips parting and answering what he was asking.

When she slid her arms around his waist, he didn't even feel the pain that shot through his side. It was hard to differentiate the agony from the ecstasy flowing through him. He was hot, all over, and every reasonable thought fell away. He could only feel.

He pulled her onto his lap, and her curves melded into his angles as they kissed. He didn't know if he was the one exploring her mouth or she his, but it was as if everything else had disappeared and ceased to matter except for the two of them. He touched her and was lost.

Her soft and smooth skin, her hair that was like a waterfall of satin, the slope of her waist, the curve of her hips.

When her hands slid down his bare chest to his waist, he felt as if he'd been scorched by a bonfire.

"Cora," he gasped, pulling away to catch his breath.

Her eyes opened, a hazy green.

Despite the fact that every muscle in his body was both aching in pain from his injuries and aching in longing for her, he couldn't allow himself to be the reason for her kingdom's neglect.

He smoothed back the hair that had fallen over her forehead.

"Don't worry about me," he said. "That kiss will keep me a young man for a long time."

She let out a light laugh. "When you look into a brass mirror, you'll see that your aging isn't what you think it is." She ran her hands up his chest and stopped at his shoulders.

It took all his self-control not to kiss her again, because he knew if he started again, he wouldn't be able to stop.

"But the fountain was polluted," he said.

Her fingers lightly tapped the base of his neck. "The water cleared after Swan's death, so I forced some into your mouth." She lifted a shoulder. "Only time will tell."

Hope rose in him. Perhaps the water would work. Perhaps he could see his family again.

"But you are right, Leo," she said, her voice low. "I must return to my father. I've dallied long enough." She lifted her hands from his skin and reached behind her.

Unclasping one of the chains about her neck, she lifted a necklace with a small stone dangling from the silver links. "Wear this, and I will know where you are."

His pulse drummed like mad as she slid the chain around his neck and clasped it behind him. The stone settled just below his collarbone, and it was warm from Cora's body heat.

"You can find me, but how will I find you?" he whispered.

She traced a finger along his jaw line. "Don't find me, Leo. My father was right. Immortals do not belong with mortals. But I wanted just a few moments to pretend that we could be together."

Then she leaned forward and kissed him. A goodbye kiss, over much too soon. And when she drew away this time, Leo knew she was really leaving.

"Get well," she whispered, then rose to her feet. She drew her cloak about her and picked up the scythe from where she must have set it on the floor when she'd come into the room.

And then, like a vanishing dream, she left.

In her wake she left only memories, and Leo wondered if it had happened at all.

Fourteen

I find my father in the meadow. He has waited for me after all, as I hoped he would, and as he has planned all along. Despite my apparent fascination with the mortal prince, my father knows that the centuries of royal blood running through me will win in the end.

When I approach, I wonder if my father can see my sorrow over leaving Leo. And I wonder if my father can see that I've been thoroughly kissed. Just the thought of it makes me feel breathless and hot.

But Leo knows as well as I that mortals and immortals must stay in their separate realms.

My father's gaze searches my face as I near, and I hope I have given nothing away.

"He lives, then?" my father asks.

"He lives," I say. "The healer predicts a short recovery, perhaps only a few days. And then he'll likely see his family."

My father's brows arch. "Has the Fountain of Youth water worked, then?"

"He looks older, but not ancient like you," I say, trying to keep my tone light. For I do not want my father to know that my heart is breaking. He deserves a pure heir to the throne, one who will make him proud. Now that Swan is dead, only the two of us remain.

My father's lips curve into a smile, and he wraps an arm about my shoulders. "Come now, we have work to do." He kisses the top of my head. "You are strong already. The reapers will respect that, and our kingdom will soon be restored and even better than before."

My eyes burn with tears, but we are already walking toward the portal. Inside a copse of trees, I link arms with my father. My last vision of earth before we transition to the Underworld is a butterfly flitting aimlessly through the meadow, as if it has all the time in the world to fly about and explore.

As the vortex draws me into the gray, I envy the butterfly. So free, so aimless, so peaceful.

I close my eyes against the gray, trying to remember all that happened in the healing room with Leo. The way his dark blue eyes looked at me as if he could see into my very heart and hear my very thoughts. The roughness of his warm hand against mine. The way he smiled when he slowly kissed me as if he were half in a delicious dream. The way his arms had cocooned my body and how I felt with his hands touching me. Safe, warm, protected, and wanting more.

The gray dissipates, and the temperature turns sharp. We've arrived in the Underworld, but we haven't transported to the portal by the throne room and all its dead. We've arrived in the king's private chamber. I have heard of a portal in my father's rooms but have never been through it.

My father lifts a heavy curtain, and the dimness is flooded with a soft red light. When I've visited my father's chambers, I've always been struck with the feeling of power mixed with respect. Now, however, as I step into the chamber, a darkness seems to infuse the room.

I realize it's because Swan had taken over these quarters when he'd imprisoned my father. The hanging tapestries look old and dusty. The thick rugs are threadbare, and I wonder how the items in the room can become so dingy so quickly. Or perhaps I've never noticed it until now.

I turn to look at my father, who is standing before a painting of the three of us—my mother, my father, and me as an infant. My mother didn't live through her pregnancy with me, but my father still had her painted into the portrait.

I used to think it was strange when I learned this detail, but now I find the portrait comforting.

My father says nothing for a long time as I continue to look about the room, noticing the cracked and worn furniture, the twice-patched upholstery, and the crumbling of the stone hearth.

"Has this room always looked like this?" I ask, breaking into the silence.

My father turns. I expect to see surprise on his face, or perhaps hear some mundane reply. Instead, he says, "There are some things I haven't told you, Cora. We should sit down."

I blink away the fear that floods through me and sit in a ratty upholstered chair across from him. His bulk is too large for his chair, but the look is so serious on his face that I don't attempt to suggest we go to the throne room. There are probably still dead immortals in there.

"The reapers have been rebelling for much longer than the takeover by Swan," he says. "It has been going on for more than a decade. Not only have I been transporting the souls of the leaders of the earth, but I've also been transporting others."

"Others?" I ask, finally finding my voice.

He nods, and suddenly I see that the worn lines about his face are not from reaching the end of his reign but from carrying a too-heavy burden.

"How many, Father?" I ask, sitting stiffly in my chair.

He hesitates, and in that hesitation, I feel another jolt of fear.

"Father, what's going on?" I rise from my chair and cross to him. Kneeling before him, I grasp his hand. "I must know all of it. I am your heir."

His black eyes focus on me, and I see that they are rimmed in red as if he's been crying. But my father is Master Grim, and he does not cry.

"All of them, Cora," he says in the faintest voice. "I have been transporting all the souls of the world."

I cannot move, cannot speak. "How is that possible? There is not enough time for one reaper to do all the work."

"I have taken more than one at a time on occasion," my father says. "But that causes problems at the Judgment."

I can only imagine. Souls are not always easy to hold on to. The strength and energy required to transport them is tremendous, let alone two at once, as well as multiple souls per day or night. When a soul reaches the Judgment, the acceptance of eternal salvation or eternal damnation does not always go smoothly. Sometimes the reaper needs to forcibly deliver the soul to its destination.

For several moments, I do not speak as I try to absorb all that my father has told me. "We need to bring the reapers together and command that they get back to work."

"Yes," my father says, absently touching my hand. "If it were that easy, I would have done it long before."

"Why can't we do that?" I ask, genuinely confused.

"Because, dear daughter," my father says in a low voice, "the corruptions run too deep now. With a lot of work, a lot of bribery, we might get a few dozen on our side."

While a few dozen is better than none, we need all the reapers. "Swan is gone now," I say, desperation filling me up. "Surely it will be possible to get more than that."

My father shakes his head, then closes his eyes. He is pale—paler than I've ever seen him, even after he came out of the prison and carried Leo to the portal.

"I'm afraid I have more bad news," he says, his eyes still shut.

Why isn't he looking at me? How much worse can the news be?

"I am losing my power," my father says in the quietest of voices. "The years spent transporting souls has worn me down. I've tried to hang on as long as I could—

to give you time to grow up. I hoped that Swan wouldn't start the rebellion so soon. I wanted you stronger, ready..."

I grasp both of his hands. "What are you saying, Father?"

He opens his eyes to look at me, but there is a long moment where he doesn't move or speak.

"I am dying," he says.

Fifteen

Leo stared into the brass mirror, just as Cora had suggested. She was right. He looked to be a man in his mid-thirties, but no older. He could possibly pass for a man in his late twenties. Lifting a hand to his jaw, he brushed against his whiskers. The healer had shaved him more than once, and this morning she'd declared that he was fit enough to travel.

That thought didn't give him as much comfort as he expected. He was still a prince, but he was no longer the youth his mother and father would recognize.

Leo had done nothing but drink broth, take whatever pasty concoctions the woman handed him, and think of Cora. And that kiss. He still burned when he thought of the way she'd touched him and kissed him back with every bit of feeling that he could ever imagine.

She'd left his side four days ago, and every moment

he'd been awake, he'd thought of her. He felt angry at being so helpless. She had to restore her kingdom, and all he could do was lie on a mat in a hut somewhere. He'd dreamed of her every moment he'd slept, making him wake up longing for her even more. He touched the chain about his neck, thinking of the moment she gave it to him.

"Ma'am?" Leo said, walking out of the room and into the corridor. The healer had refused to tell him her name. She'd said it was for his own protection, which he didn't entirely understand. She'd also told him he needed to leave her hut when night fell and to not talk to anyone he might meet in the village.

Leo could do that.

But before he left, he had questions.

"Ma'am?" he said again.

The corridor was dim, and he thought he heard a child's laugh. The healer had mentioned a child a time or two, but Leo hadn't seen her. Besides, it must be a grandchild, because the healer was older than any natural mother would be.

He shuffled through the corridor, limping slightly, but he was grateful to be upright and walking at last.

At one end of the corridor, a door stood open.

"There you are," the healer's voice croaked as he stepped through the open doorway. The room he'd entered had several windows in it, letting in the afternoon light from outside. Leo hadn't seen the sun for days.

The walls were lined with hooks, and it appeared that herbs and plants were hanging from them and drying.

The healer stepped out from a stack of crates. Her

wizened gaze made a quick study of his features. "You are looking well, my prince."

The only reason he knew he was in Navarre was because this woman deferred to him as royalty.

Then, a small head poked out from behind the healer's skirts. The young girl giggled.

"Go play with your doll," the healer said, steering the girl away.

The child scampered past Leo and out of the room.

"Is that your..."

His voice trailed perhaps a bit too long, because the healer waved away his question and didn't answer it. "You've come for money?"

Leo shook his head. "Money? No, I've no need—"

"Everyone has need of money," the healer said. "Even a lost prince." She walked over to a nearby table and lifted the lid of a wooden box.

"Really, I don't want your money," Leo said.

The woman chuckled and released the lid. "You're a foolish man," she said, folding her arms. "It will take you two days to reach your father's palace."

"I just need a bit of bread and cheese."

The woman opened the lid of the box again. "The queen said you were stubborn, so she left you this." The healer lifted out a pouch, and by the shape of it, Leo guessed it was filled with coins.

Curiosity won out, and Leo stepped forward to take the pouch. He opened it and was surprised to see raw gemstones mixed in with several coins.

The healer smiled. "I suppose she thought a prince couldn't travel without a pouch of jewels."

"This is very generous," Leo said, looking into the old woman's eyes. "But not necessary. Here,"—he handed the pouch over—"take it as payment for your care."

The healer waved him off. "I've been paid well. You will need those jewels in your travels." By the way her eyes gleamed as she spoke, Leo had the sense the jewels were not an ordinary commodity.

He removed one out of the pouch and turned it over so that it caught the light. The gem was a deep purple and reminded Leo of the amulet about Master Fate's neck before he used it to kill Swan.

"What do you know about the . . . queen . . . who visited me?" he asked in a slow voice.

The healer folded her arms. "Mistress Grim? I thought you'd been delirious when you spoke of her, but then she appeared." The woman lifted her shoulders in a shrug. "I don't know how you got mixed up with her, but I appreciated the business she brought me. And I hope that my services will keep me free of the likes of her for a good long while. She told me some things about the Underworld and how you came to be injured. I must confess, after she left, I dug out my book of legends. It seems the storybook legends are not too far off."

"Do you know what her powers are?" he asked. "We both agree she is the Mistress of Death, and although I haven't been a believer in sorcery, it seems I was wrong."

The healer let out a raspy chuckle. "It doesn't matter whether or not you believe in sorcery. It's there, regardless. I've seen it, and I've even used it a time or two, but I prefer to use what nature has provided. And believe me, the queen who came to check on you is not mortal."

"What do you know of Queen Cora then? What does your book of legends tell you?"

"Cora . . . It makes sense that is her name. She is the daughter of the Grim Reaper. She is the heir to the Underworld. So it bodes well to steer clear of her kind."

"What would happen if I seek her out?" Leo asked.

The healer's thin eyebrows rose. "She is an immortal. And you can see what happened to you when you were in her realm. You wouldn't last a single moon down there. You would be an old man before you know it."

Leo rubbed at the whiskers on his face. "Cora said the Fountain of Youth would help."

"Giving the water to you would be dangerous," the healer said. "If people on earth learned of its existence, just think of the wars that would be started."

"I could live in the Underworld then," Leo said.

The healer's chuckle was dry. "Your rapid aging and the water from the Fountain of Youth would constantly be at odds with each other. You'd look like an old man with a spring in his step."

The image might have been funny if it didn't apply to him.

The healer shuffled closer to Leo as if she had something important to say. "The best thing you can do is forget your infatuation with Lady Death," she breathed out. "Even if she is in love with you and is willing to risk the Underworld's delicate balance to bring a mortal into her realm, the others won't accept a mortal king as her mate—even for the few decades you manage to live down there."

Leo stepped back. This woman was making a lot of

assumptions, although, deep down, she was answering his most basic questions. "I don't plan to upset the Underworld . . . I just wondered what the rules are."

"The rules?" The woman cackled like a witch out of a storybook. "The rules are that mortals and immortals should not mix. Ever. Your father is alive. Be grateful for that." She raised a finger and would have jabbed it in his chest if Leo hadn't taken another step back. "Stay away from Lady Death, my prince. No infatuation or professed love is worth throwing the world into chaos. For if you pursue her, mark my words, the very minions of hell will come after you."

Leo exhaled. "Cora can travel between her realm and earth easily," he said. "What if I stay here and she visits me?"

The healer shook her head. "That is no life. And she will need an heir, an immortal heir."

Leo didn't say anything for a moment. "Can I see your book of legends?"

The woman didn't seem surprised at his request. She aimed her finger toward a table in the corner. The table was littered with scrolls and what looked to be old manuscripts. In the middle was a leather-bound book.

Leo crossed the room and looked down at the book. Etched into the leather, the title read: *Legends of the Damned*.

He opened the thick cover. He started to read the first lines of the handwritten scrawl: *The account of Sir Jeppson when he visited the Underworld, transcribed on his deathbed.*

Leo turned page after page and studied the drawings

that depicted all kinds of creatures. Two of them looked like reapers. Leo slowed his perusal and read through the text below the drawings.

The reapers will transport your soul to Judgment. At the Judgment, the Fates will decide where your soul will spend eternity. Those who interfere with a reaper's work will lose their own soul in the process. Perhaps not right away, but the time of reckoning will come. Only one person has ever conquered a reaper. In the twelfth century, Lady Jane White claimed to have visited the Underworld realm. She claimed to have married the king, who we call the Grim Reaper, and she had his child. When she returned to her village, after only being away for one year, she'd transformed into an old woman.

Physicians verified that she indeed had given birth to a child, but she had left the child behind. On her deathbed, she kept trying to rise and return to the Underworld. She was deemed insane and kept locked in her bedchamber until the day of her death.

Leo knew that Lady Jane White was not insane. For if she was, then he was too.

Sixteen

My father's words rock through me. He says he's dying, and he says that the reapers have been rebelling for decades. My father has shouldered a tremendous burden all by himself for much too long. And now it's killing him.

I reach for his hand again in the stillness of his chamber. I don't like the defeat in his expression. "I can work day and night to transport the souls," I say. "You regain your strength and then work on recruiting reapers to help me."

My heart is thundering with anxiety. So many souls are trapped in their decaying corpses. I must find a way. So much time has passed.

But my father hasn't responded to me. It's as if he's already given up. His eyes remain closed, but I know he isn't sleeping. Anger surges through me. How dare the reapers turn against their duties?

I leave my father's side, pick up the scythe, and barge out of his chambers. In the corridor, I find more destructtion and decay. It's as if the Underworld itself is dying. I hurry to the commons. The Fountain of Youth is still clear, and this at least brings me relief. But there is no one to guard it. The sirens are gone, and I must first secure the fountain.

I find a group of reapers in the purple corridor where Master Swan used to live. Their scowls when I enter tell me enough of my challenge. They will not harm me, at least not as long as my father is around, but what might happen if they find out how weak he is?

Since there are only about seven of them, I say, "If you are still loyal to Swan, you are banished to the outer realm."

One of the reapers actually snarls at me like a beast. I recognize her as Beaux. We have never been friends, and now I know why. I lift my scythe. I will not relish destroying reapers that can be of help, but I need to stop the dissension somewhere.

The reaper who snarled takes a step toward me, but a quick glance at the others tells me that they are not all in agreement with the first reaper. Still, seven to one is manageable. I've been well trained, and my scythe has the power to kill another reaper. Their scythes are not as strong.

Beaux continues to advance as if she might intimidate me. Her thick brown hair is braided over her shoulder, and if not for the intensity of her expression, she would be a pretty immortal.

The other six reapers also move forward, but I don't see menace in their expressions. It seems that Beaux is the leader of this small group.

I don't wait for her to strike first.

I lunge and swing the scythe at her neck, but she's quick and moves out of the way.

I am quick too. I'm also angry. I swing again, and the scythe connects with her upper arm. She howls, then spins away. I am right behind her, and I raise the scythe over my head and bring it down on top of her shoulder.

She crumples to the ground with a second howl, then goes quiet.

I almost don't believe I've defeated her. But I cannot check, for there are six more reapers in the corridor.

I turn, gripping the scythe before me, ready to strike at my next foe.

The six reapers have stopped in their tracks and are staring at their fallen leader.

No one speaks for several moments. Then, to my astonishment, one by one, each reaper sinks to his or her knees and bows their heads.

They are offering their allegiance to me, but I hesitate. Can I fully trust these six reapers? If so, at least it's a start.

"Follow me," I say to the bowed heads. They rise to their feet, and we pass by the fallen reaper. Her body in the corridor will serve as a warning to others.

I lead them to the fountain and assign one of them to guard it. Then I continue to the throne room. We're almost bowled over by the stench of the dead bodies. At least Master Fate and the prince had moved them to one side of the room. I stop by the broken oval table where my father used to hold his council meetings. Etched into the center of the table used to be a map of the earth. Now, that too is rent in half.

I look at the reapers who've followed me. "What are your names?" Each of them gives me a name. They are familiar, although as far as I can remember I have not interacted with these reapers.

"Here," I say, pointing at the map of Asia, then looking at one of the reapers—a young male name Cernan. "You will start here. You may need to transport more than one soul at a time. We are woefully behind."

He nods, and I can see by the steady gaze in his eyes that he is ready to work.

"Go now," I continue. "We cannot delay."

Cernan enters the portal, and I turn to the others, giving them assignments. Until I can recruit more reapers, we'll all be working day and night to transport souls.

Once the six have gone into the portal, I hurry into the red corridor. Several doors down, I walk into my father's personal chamber to find him still in the chair before the hearth. He has fallen asleep like a mortal. I stand before him, not moving. I am stunned at his decline in health. I don't remember ever seeing my father sleep.

I approach and kneel next to him once again. When I touch his hand, his eyes drag open. I explain about the six reapers, and a small smile touches his lips.

"I need to get more on our side," I continue. "But I can't fight them all."

My father gives a slight nod. "The Fates," he says. "Consult with the Fates." And then his eyes shut.

"Father," I say, grasping his arm. "Wake up." I press my fingers against his neck. His pulse is still steady and warm, and he is breathing. But fear has gripped me tight.

Then I have an idea. I look about my father's chamber to find a vase, and I grab it, then rush to the Fountain of Youth. I scoop up a vaseful of the water, then return to my father's side. I bathe his face in the water and then dribble some into his mouth. I wait several moments, but nothing changes.

Finally, I decide that I must seek out the Fates as my father has asked. I must plead for their help.

Leo read through the text again in the light of the small fire he'd built in the middle of the forest. He'd been traveling for days . . . wandering, more like it. He had the text in the book of legends memorized now. Nothing was new, of course, but he continued to study it.

His appearance was too changed to return to his father's palace. His mother would have a fit when she saw him. They'd probably try to hold an exorcism. And after reading about Lady Jane White, Leo didn't want to put his parents through such an ordeal.

Besides, he'd checked his reflection in the taverns where he'd stayed overnight, and he hadn't grown any older, nor younger. He did notice he was earning more respect by appearing as a full-grown man, and that was without letting people know that he was the heir to the new throne of Navarre. He didn't need word about his changed appearance to reach his parents.

The words in the leather-bound book flickered in the glow of the firelight, and still Leo had no answers. He idly turned the rest of the pages, then stopped at an image he hadn't paid much attention to before. It was that of a sea mermaid. About her neck she wore a strand of jewels. But the jewels weren't ordinary.

Leo peered closer at the image. The jewels didn't have plain faces, but symbols had been carved into them. Leo's pulse quickened. The symbols were familiar. What if... He withdrew the pouch of jewels the healer had given to him. He opened the pouch and dumped a couple of the gemstones onto his palm.

The orange glow of the flames created shadows that Leo hadn't seen before, and he realized these jewels had been carved as well. Comparing the drawing in the book and the jewels in his palm, he found that the symbols were the same.

His mind raced. Were these jewels duplicates? Or were they the actual jewels from the illustration?

Leo began to read the text, titled "Legend of Sevena." The mermaid had fallen in love with a mortal—a fairy tale Leo had heard more than once—but she didn't find a way to live on land. Instead, the man came to live with her beneath the sea. As long as he wore the Sevena necklace, he could breathe underwater.

Leo read through the text again, and then a third time. Finally he tucked the book into his satchel and gathered up his belongings. He had an idea, and he knew he wouldn't be able to rest until he tried it. First, he had to find a jeweler who could add the gems to the necklace Cora had given him.

Leo traveled through the night, sleep a thing of his past life. Sometimes he felt as if he were in a dream. With the jewels in his possession and determination in his mind, by the time the sun crested the eastern horizon, he'd arrived at a small town on the coast.

The sea air was sharp and brisk, blowing in on a steady breeze. Fishing boats that looked like they'd been anchored along the shore during the night were bustling with early activity as the fishermen prepared for another day of casting their nets and hooks.

The pungent scent caused Leo's stomach to clench. He was both hungry and repelled by the smell of fish entrails on the rocky shoreline. The gulls were making quick work of any tidbits.

Leo caught a whiff of baking bread mixed in with the scent of fish. His stomach practically dragged him to the bakery one lane up from the seaside.

He'd never been so grateful as he was for the handful of coins that the healer had given him. He hurried to the shop, bought a couple of buns, then asked the round-faced baker if there was a jeweler in the town.

The baker eyed him carefully. "You have a repair to make?"

"No, I need to add colored glass to a necklace I already have," Leo hedged.

"My daughter can make simple creations," the baker said. "Violette!" he shouted.

Leo flinched at the man's sudden yell.

A scrawny girl who looked to be about eleven came running into the shop.

Leo was already shaking his head before the baker could speak. He didn't want his necklace to resemble some child's play at making a flower chain.

The baker placed his thick hand on the girl's knobby shoulders. "Violette has done repair work for royalty."

Leo doubted it, but he listened anyway.

"She's quite skilled at managing simple jobs," the baker said.

"I need work done on a necklace," Leo said, looking at the young girl. "I cannot entrust this work to a beginner, no matter how skilled. Who taught you?"

The girl looked up at her father as if seeking his permission to speak.

"Go on ahead," the baker said in a gruff voice. "You can take him to Ma."

"Her mother is a jeweler?" Leo asked.

"Hush," the baker said, glancing out the shop windows. "Follow her out the back door."

Leo didn't need to be told twice. He hurried after the thin girl and stepped through a doorway that led outside into a walled courtyard. The girl looked over her shoulder at him, as if to make sure he followed, then she darted through a gate.

Leo continued through the gate and was surprised to see a small house. It had been completely hidden when he approached the bakery. The girl opened the front door and ushered him inside. Then she spoke the first words Leo had heard her speak.

"Ma. We have a patron."

There was no answering reply, but the girl didn't seem bothered by it. She pushed aside a curtain that separated the room into two halves. Leo followed and saw a woman who was probably only in her thirties but looked much older. No, she was deformed. It appeared as if she'd been severely burned. She wore a cloak that covered much of her head, but her face was exposed. The red, lumpy skin looked painful. Leo had a hard time keeping his gaze on her. He wanted to both gape and turn away.

"Welcome," the woman said through lips that were unnaturally red. Her voice had a high, reedy quality. "What is it you need?"

Leo exhaled and glanced about the room. The woman's disfigurement had fully captured his attention, but now that he looked around, he saw high, narrow tables filled with jewelry-making tools, and several velvet-lined boxes displayed intricate gold and silver necklaces and bracelets, and there was even a crown. Leo stared.

"Ah, you like it?" the woman said. She rose and crossed to the high table, where she lifted the crown from its velvet cocoon. "It's over a hundred years old. I restored it to its full luster."

"Who did it belong to?" Leo asked, trying not to focus on the woman's marred skin.

"Queen Eleanor," she said.

Leo had never heard of a Queen Eleanor, but he wasn't here to learn about history. The display proved that this woman could make jewelry.

"I need a necklace added to," he said, reaching for the pouch in his satchel.

The woman watched him pick out the gemstones. She picked one off his palm and turned it over. When the symbol caught the light in the room, she gasped.

"I cannot," she said, setting the gem firmly onto his palm again. She turned to her daughter, who was lingering in the room. "Go and feed the chickens." The young girl scampered out of the room.

"Ma'am," Leo started. "Surely you have the skill to fix these jewels into my chain."

"These gems have otherworldly power in them," the woman said in a hushed voice. "I cannot have them in my home. Just their presence will put my family in danger."

Leo didn't know if this woman was mad or sane. "What kind of danger?"

The woman looked past him as if she expected someone to enter the room at any moment. Then, in a low voice she said, "Once these jewels are set into a necklace, the creatures of the shadows will be attracted to the town. You are probably being followed now. You must leave and never come back."

Leo stared at her. Whatever he'd sensed about these gemstones in connection with the mermaid story had to have substance. Which was why he needed this woman's help. "How long will it take to complete a simple necklace?" He motioned toward the worktable. "I'll give you all the coin in my pouch. And . . . then I'll tell you a secret that cannot be shared with anyone."

The woman hesitated. With her deformity, surely she didn't go out into the town much, and she must enjoy a secret as much as any recluse. "If my daughter comes back, she must not come into this room. I'll not have her lay eyes upon the gemstones. She will be marked if she does."

"Agreed," Leo said, handing over the pouch to the woman. Then he removed the chain about his neck and handed that over too.

"Give these coins to my husband," she said, "and tell him I must work in absolute silence. He will understand."

Leo nodded. He left the woman at the worktable and went out of the house. Once he reached the bakery, he handed over the coins to the baker.

The man didn't seem surprised when Leo told him the instructions from his wife.

"And my daughter is assisting her?" the baker asked with a bit of pride in his tone.

"She is feeding the chickens," Leo said.

"Ah," the baker said. "When you see her, tell her I need her help in the shop again."

Leo nodded and went out into the courtyard again. He didn't see the little girl, so he went into the house, knocking on the door before opening it. He made his way to the workroom.

The baker's wife didn't even look up as he entered. She was focused on inlaying the stones into silver clamps. He sat across from her and watched, caught up in her handiwork. She worked quickly and deftly as the sunlight spilled into the room, making everything glow bright.

Once she had all the gemstones inlaid, she began to attach them to a silver chain. When the second to last jewel was attached, the light dimmed in the room. Leo glanced out of the window to see dark clouds had built up in the sky.

A peal of thunder startled Leo. The morning had been clear, and there hadn't been a single cloud over the sea when he arrived in town.

The baker's wife finally looked up, distracted by the sound of the thunder. "Oh no," she whispered. She wiped at her face, then turned back to her work.

"What is it?"

"They've tracked the jewels," the woman muttered.

A ripple of fear swept through Leo. "Who? And how?"

"I told you, they have otherworldly power," the woman said without lifting her head to look at him. "Once assembled like I am doing, they become a mark."

Another rumble of thunder rippled through the sky. This one was followed by a sharp streak of lightning. Raindrops started to fall, first in a soft patter, then stronger until the sound turned into a dull roar.

"There," the woman said, picking up the necklace and holding it toward Leo. "Take it and run. Leave this place as fast as you can."

Leo took the necklace. It was heavy and sturdy, and if the sun came out again, it would shine in brilliance. He could hardly believe the sudden storm outside was caused by these jewels. But the baker's wife looked as if she'd been standing inside a hot furnace. Perspiration dripped from her face, and she was breathing like she'd run across the entire town in mere seconds.

"Go," she said, pushing at his arm. A clap of thunder drowned out all sound for an instant. When it settled, the baker's wife screeched, "Go!"

Leo grabbed the satchel he'd left on the table and rushed out of the room. The courtyard was becoming a muddy torrent of rain, and Leo splashed through the water. Moments later, he'd passed the baker's shop and started running down the muddy lane.

Thunder boomed overhead, and lightning streaked across the deep purple sky. Not a dozen paces ahead, lightning struck a broad oak tree. The trunk split in half with a massive groan.

Leo's heart nearly stopped.

And then the necklace seemed to tug away from his grasp. Leo tightened his grip, but still the necklace pulled. It was leading him directly toward the blackened tree. Leo wrapped both hands around the chain. He stumbled against the roots of the tree as the necklace pulled him.

Suddenly, it was as if Leo had stepped off the edge of a cliff, and earth disappeared beneath his feet.

There was nothing below him.

And he started to fall.

Seventeen

The Judgment is located on an oasis, a field of green where the Fates stand in a semicircle, their long, pale robes floating about their feet. Surrounding the oasis is a sea of thick mist that falls into a nothingness. The only way a soul can arrive at Judgment is to be brought in by a reaper.

By the time I arrive, there are two reapers before me—my new recruits. I am pleased to see them. One of them is Cernan, the other a female reaper named Augustine. Cernan is wrestling with containing three souls, and I am impressed by his fortitude. If one of the souls escapes his grasp, they will float into limbo for the rest of eternity.

Augustine only has one soul with her, who seems to be behaving. I am disappointed that she didn't attempt to bring a second. At this rate, the number of souls trapped in their dead bodies will only continue to rise.

Seeing the five Fates reminds me of the loss of Master Fate and of his sacrifice. I feel humbled, and I wish that he hadn't needed to give up his immortality on my behalf.

One of Cernan's souls is judged, and the Fate escorts the compliant soul into the mist. I wait for the second soul to receive Judgment, and I can't help listening in.

"Jonathan Revere, you have lived a good life," the Fate pronounces.

The soul stops its trembling at that news.

"You have cared for your wife and children," the Fate continues. "You have kept your vices at bay. You will receive glory for eternity."

The soul seems to straighten. The Fate steps forward and motions for the soul to follow him into the mist.

Next, Cernan presents the third soul. This one struggles against Cernan, and he holds on tight. The soul doesn't receive such a peaceful fate.

"Genevieve Saunders," the Fate begins. "You have lived a life of greed and whoredom with no remorse. You have been condemned to the second depth of hell."

The soul howls and tries to escape the reaper's hold.

But Cernan is strong, and the Fate easily grasps the other side of what used to be Genevieve Saunders. She is half dragged into the mists, and like a candle blown out, her cries cut off.

Cernan has spotted me, and he moves to my side.

We both watch as Augustine presents her soul. A young child who is more frightened than aware of his Judgment. Without a sound from him, he accepts his glory and leaves with one of the Fates.

When Augustine sees me, her eyes narrow.

"Bring two or three souls next time," I say in an even tone. She doesn't blink, but at least she nods.

She leaves, and I turn to Cernan, who is still standing by me. "Can you recruit more reapers?" I ask.

"Where is your soul?" one of the Fate's voices booms out.

I turn to face a Fate who is more than a head taller than me. "My father is dying," I say without any preamble. "Swan's rebellion continues even without his presence. I need more reapers to swear allegiance to me."

The Fates are silent for a moment.

"They need a leader," one of the Fates says.

"My father was their leader, yet they turned away from him," I counter.

"Swan persuaded them," the Fate says. "You must persuade them back."

"This is why I've come to you," I say. "Tell me how to gain control of the Underworld."

When none of the Fates answer, Cernan says, "What about the law of the sacrifice?"

I turn to him. I have heard of this ancient law, but I am not sure how it applies here. Religions throughout the ancient civilizations believed that an animal, or sometimes even mortals, could be sacrificed to unify their people or to appease a god. Different sacrifices were implemented, from sin sacrifices to peace sacrifices.

A sin sacrifice was when an animal would be butchered as a scapegoat and as cleansing for a crime committed by a mortal. A peace sacrifice would be done before an important event such as a royal marriage or before entering into a war.

None of the Fates look particularly pleased with Cernan's suggestion. But I am intrigued. "Tell me of this law and how it will save my kingdom."

Cernan glances at the circle of Fates, but since none of them seem ready to offer guidance, he says, "You will pledge a sacrifice that will cost you dear. The sacrifice will prove your loyalty to the Underworld. Those who accept your oath will be bound by their own immortal lives to pledge allegiance to you, and the blood of the sacrifice will keep them bound to you. They cannot back out or change their minds. They will be bound for eternity."

I exhale. "Has this been done before?" I think over my lessons from Swan and over the conversations with my father. I have not heard of such a thing on this large of a scale. We are talking about the entire Underworld here.

"No," the Fates say in unison.

I look at Cernan. "Then how do I know it will work?"

His gaze is intelligent, determined, and steady. "It will work, but only if the sacrifice is a true sacrifice from your heart."

"True," I repeat.

"Cernan is right," one of the Fates says. "But your father is dying, and the Underworld will not accept the sacrifice of the already ill-fated."

That means the only sacrifice that will bring the kingdom under my rule is Leo.

The Fates and Cernan are all watching me, waiting for my answer.

I turn away from Cernan's knowing gaze. How much does he know? Surely all the Underworld knows about the prince who fought for me. Surely they all know that my father is dying. There must be another way.

I look at the circle of Fates. "I will do what I must, but is there another choice?"

"Mortal or immortal, the life of another is the ultimate sacrifice," one of the Fates says. "The sacrifice will fulfill the law, and the law will be the foundation of your power."

The prince is but a mortal—a mortal who already owes me his soul for saving his father's life. During my first sojourn to earth I met Leo. Although I am innocent, I realize that I may encounter other mortals that I feel this pull toward.

Even as I try to convince myself of this, I know that even though I may be young for an immortal, I have gone too far down the path with Leo. I have allowed myself to bond.

Because of this, I will be heartbroken to bring such a fate upon Leo, but it must be done. The sacrifice will produce so much more than Leo living out his mortal life of . . . what? Running away from his duty as the king of Navarre's heir? Spending his days hunting? Perhaps finding a wife and raising a family, only to die one day and have his soul come to Judgment?

I will just be speeding up his Judgment day. No mortal can escape it.

I feel as if I have aged a century when I look Cernan in the eyes, then each of the Fates in turn. "I will make the sacrifice." I feel as if my heart has turned to stone with my words. "Meanwhile, Cernan," I say in a pointed voice, even though I'd rather seclude myself in a dark room somewhere so that I don't have to feel or see anything but my own shadow. "Recruit who you can. The work must go on until I can take control of the kingdom."

Cernan gives me the slightest nod, and I wonder if he doubted me or if he predicted what I might say.

I have to be by myself now. I need to mull over my promise, and even though I know I will not go back on my word, I can't breathe with the Fates and Cernan watching me.

I must go to my father. I must make a plan.

I leave the Judgment and transport back to the Underworld. In the gray of the vortex, I notice something in the distance. Normally there is nothing but gray, but a dark form contrasts with the swirling dullness. It's not a reaper, because it would be rare for us to be in the same portal at the same time.

I move closer to the form and realize my pulse has sped up. I am not afraid, but I am unsure.

Then the form turns slightly as if it's floating without any control over its motions.

Leo.

I stare, and then I am moving faster. His eyes are closed, but he appears to be breathing, although his paleness makes me wonder.

I cannot help the way my heart leaps and how I consider for one moment that perhaps I will go back on my word. I can transition to earth and live as a mortal. My life would end within a few decades, like all mortals' do, but I would be with Leo.

The fact that he's floating in the vortex tells me that he came to find me. Somehow he entered a portal on his own. I've never seen it done, and I know that he cannot reach a destination by himself; he needs the help of an immortal. So the fact that he risked his life to enter the portal tells me something else.

He returns my feelings.

The feelings I refuse to name.

"Leo," I whisper as I grasp his arm to stop his aimless turning. "What have you done?"

And then I see it. A silver chain about his neck, studded with gemstones. They aren't ordinary gems; they are the ones I left with the healer.

He has figured out the legend.

My heart drops again. He has come for me, and here I am, ready to sacrifice him for my kingdom.

Eighteen

Leo awakened in a room of red. Everything was red, from the ceiling to the tapestries to the walls peeking out behind the tapestries, to the armchair next to the bed, to the red tunic he wore.

He sat up, too quickly it turned out, and his head protested with an angry burst of pain.

"How are you feeling?" a deep voice asked.

Leo turned his head to see the Grim Reaper himself sprawled out on a chair on the opposite side of the bed.

"I—I'm alive," Leo said, as lame as it sounded.

It looked like the Grim Reaper almost smiled, if the twisting of his dark lips was an indicator.

Leo tried to calm his erratic heartbeat. Even though he was looking at Lord Death, the man was Cora's father. He was an immortal, yes, but he was also quite comfortably sitting in this red chamber with Leo. And Leo wasn't dead yet—at least he didn't think so.

"You are alive," the Grim Reaper said. "And no small feat, if I must comment upon your state."

"Where—where am I?" Leo asked. "And what—what happened?"

The Grim Reaper steepled his very long fingers. "Ah, I thought you'd ask those questions. Why don't *you* start by telling me what happened at the healer's place?"

Leo's mind was starting to piece it all together, although he felt like chunks of his memory were missing. He began to tell the Grim Reaper—as if it were just a casual conversation between two men in a tavern—about the book of legends and the pouch of jewels.

The Grim Reaper said nothing as Leo told his tale. So Leo continued and talked about the baker, the baker's wife, and then the terrible storm. He remembered nothing after the necklace had pulled him toward the burned tree. As if he could believe in a necklace having that sort of power, but who was Leo to question? He was sitting across from a creature that was only supposed to exist in fables.

The Grim Reaper listened, and when Leo finished, he said, "Cora found you in the vortex. If she hadn't . . . you would have eventually starved to death."

A shiver ran through Leo. "I am grateful to Cora—I am in debt to her." He still wasn't clear on how he'd been drawn through the portal, but he knew it had something to do with his necklace of jewels. He touched the necklace surrounding his neck.

"You are in grievous debt," the Grim Reaper said. "But my daughter is determined to defy my advice and keep you alive. In the natural order of the Underworld, you would forfeit your life in order to pay the debt of your father's life. Cora left those jewels for you, and because you put them into a necklace and are wearing it, you are protected from the opposing forces of the Underworld."

Leo ran a hand over his face. "What does that mean?"

The Grim Reaper motioned to the wall to the left of Leo. "Look into the mirror."

Leo turned. A mirror hung on the wall, and Leo gazed at his reflection. He hadn't aged any further. "This necklace keeps me from aging?"

"Among other things," the Grim Reaper said. "I must tell you something that you cannot share with Cora. If you do, it will prove the downfall of the Underworld. You must swear that you will keep this secret."

"I will." Leo didn't exactly have a choice, but he wasn't about to contradict the Lord of Death.

"Cora will be returning to my chambers soon," the reaper started. "She is trying to reverse the damage that Swan has done over the last decade. But the corruption runs deep in the minds of the reapers. The only way she'll be able to earn their allegiance is to sacrifice what she holds most dear, whether it be mortal or immortal. Cora would have to forever banish her loved one's soul."

Leo felt the breath leave him. Cora was about to sacrifice her father in order to save the kingdom that he ruled? "You are what she holds most dear."

The Grim Reaper shook his head slowly. "No. I am at the end of my years, and the reapers know it. They would not accept a sacrifice of a dying immortal. She will need to sacrifice *you*."

Even as the Grim Reaper said the words, Leo knew it. He was already having trouble wrapping his mind around the fact that Cora might consider him so highly. But now that he knew that she must make so great a sacrifice, he decided that his mortality was not worth the price of disrupting the order of the Underworld.

"Is there no other way?" he asked.

"No."

"I will do it," he said.

"I know you will," the Grim Reaper said, and Leo thought he detected a note of pride in Death's voice. "But Cora will be harder to convince."

"What do you mean?" Leo asked. "Surely she knows this will break down the rebellion and restore order."

"Yes, but she is stubborn," the Grim Reaper said. "She presently thinks she can fight each reaper into submission. She's won over a handful so far, but there are too many rebels, and only one of her. I . . . I cannot fight any longer." He lifted his hand as if to show the weakness that had overcome him. "It is my greatest sorrow to hand over a fractured kingdom to my daughter."

"When she returns, we'll convince her," Leo said.

"I was hoping you'd say that," the Grim Reaper said. "You must be the one to convince her. It won't be easy. You must tell her that time has run out. Every moment counts. Every moment more mortals die and become trapped."

Leo exhaled. He could do this; he *would* do this. Death was but the next phase in life.

"There's one more thing," the Grim Reaper said. "The sacrifice will be real in Cora's mind, but the necklace you wear has the power to turn you into an immortal if your heart is truly turned to hers."

"How?"

The Grim Reaper exhaled. "When she sacrifices you, instead of dying a mortal death, your flesh will become immortal. Your soul will remain, and you'll become part of the Underworld. Although, this is only according to legend. I have never seen something of this magnitude take place in my lifetime."

Either way . . . whether or not the jewels worked, he was not returning to earth as a mortal.

"If I'm immortal, then Cora and I can be . . ."

"Together," her father finished.

Leo hadn't been planning on talking about this to Cora's father, but now that it was out, he was feeling more determined than ever. Obtaining immortality was more than he could hope for. And if the necklace didn't work . . . then, his life would be shorter than expected.

"But, there's a third option," the Grim Reaper said. "I transport you back to earth, and you live your life out as a mortal. Leave all the Underworld business to the rest of us."

"I will do the sacrifice," Leo said, meeting Grim's gaze. "For better or for worse."

Grim gave a brief nod, his eyes appraising Leo. "Very well. She's coming now, and your job is to convince her."

"Father," Cora's voice echoed into the room as she appeared in the doorway. "How is he . . ." She caught sight of Leo sitting up in the bed. "Oh. You're awake."

The relief on her face jolted Leo's heart. How had this beautiful immortal come to care so much for him? She wore a dress of fiery red. It cut across her shoulders, and on its way down, the dress molded to her curves, then splashed to the floor, covering her feet.

Leo swung his legs over the side of the bed to stand up. But Cora rushed toward him. "No, you should rest. You were nearly . . . dead . . . when I found you in the vortex."

Perhaps she was right, because Leo did feel like his head was spinning with the movement.

"I told him about the sacrifice, Cora," her father said, pushing to his feet. His hands shook as he drew his cloak about him. "He is willing to be the sacrifice."

"No," Cora said, whirling to face her father. "You shouldn't have told him, and you shouldn't have asked him to agree. I've defeated four more reapers, and they have pledged their allegiance to me. Three are already in the portal on their way to resume their tasks."

It was then that Leo noticed the white-knuckled grip she had on her scythe.

"How many did you have to kill to get those four?" her father asked, his expression hard.

Cora paused. "Seven."

"You lost seven to gain four," the Grim Reaper said in a slow voice. "There are three hundred reapers. At this rate, you'll lose two-thirds of them . . . and that's if you're lucky."

No one spoke for a moment. "I can do this, Father."

Her father stepped toward her, holding out his hand for his scythe.

Cora handed it over, and her father took it and lifted it up as if he was inspecting it. "This weapon isn't strong enough to take control of the kingdom. Believe me, I've been trying." His gaze cut to Leo's. "We have a much more sure option."

Cora turned from her father and walked to the hearth. She stood before it, hands clasped in front of her, head bowed. For several long moments, neither father nor daughter spoke.

Leo pushed himself to his feet. He felt as if he'd spent three days straight in battle with no food or water. But he needed to make Cora understand that it wasn't her father who'd convinced him.

"Cora," he said.

She didn't move, didn't respond.

The Grim Reaper walked toward the door, and with a final nod at Leo, he left the room.

Nineteen

Leo didn't know if her father's presence or lack of presence would make a difference. But he continued walking toward Cora. The closer he got, the more he remembered their kiss and how she felt in his arms. He wanted to tell her that he could become immortal, but he knew he couldn't or the sacrifice wouldn't be authentic.

"Cora," he whispered, placing his hands on her shoulders.

She turned suddenly and wrapped her arms about his waist. He pulled her close, resting his chin on top of her head. She was trembling, and he realized that she was crying.

"The healer had a book of legends," he started. "And when I read the legend of the mermaid, I knew that the jewels would allow me to return to you. Isn't that why you gave them to the healer? Because you wanted me to figure it out and decide what I wanted?"

"Yes," Cora whispered. "But I didn't . . ." Her voice broke. "I didn't want *this*."

"I know," Leo said, running his hand over her hair. It was finer than any royal silk. "I have nothing without you, Cora. I don't want my father's throne, and there is no other place I'd rather be than here, with you. No matter how short that time is."

Cora lifted her head to look at him. Her pale green eyes held a depth of sorrow that wrenched at Leo's heart. The only thing he'd truly miss when his soul was judged would be her.

"I can't lose you," she said.

Her breath was sweet, and Leo lowered his head. "You won't lose me. I'll still be in your memory." He ran a finger along her cheek, soaking up the stray tears that had fallen. "Besides, what's a few mortal years?"

"Leo, don't say that," she said, wrapping her arms about his neck and tugging him closer until their foreheads met and their breathing mingled. "I can find a way to save my kingdom without sacrificing you."

"Time has run out," Leo said. "Your father knows it, and you know it."

Cora's eyes slipped shut, and she released a breath. "I never asked to be the heir to the throne. I never had a choice."

"But you have a choice now," he whispered. "And I already made mine."

She lifted her chin and pressed her mouth against his.

She tasted of salty tears and sweet honey. Her kisses were hungry, demanding, and she pressed against him so that he could feel all her curves and valleys. He returned her kisses with equal fervor, and he backed her up against the tapestry-covered wall. She ran her hands over his shoulders, then down his chest.

"Leo," she gasped between kisses. "Stay with me tonight. Just one night."

He lifted his head, his breathing coming fast. "We don't have time," he said. "Your father said—"

"I'll make the time," Cora shot back. "I need you, and I want you to know how sorry I am." Her gaze held his, and Leo knew he might damn himself, but he couldn't say no to her.

He scooped her up in his arms and walked toward the massive red-blanketed bed. She clung to him as her hair cascaded over one arm. He could see the pulse in her neck beating like mad.

He bent to kiss her neck, tasting the sweetness of her skin.

One night, he told himself. The Underworld couldn't completely disintegrate in only one night. He set her onto the covers, and she pulled him with her. He tumbled onto the bed next to her, and she started to tug off his clothing, lifting the tunic to expose his bare stomach. It came completely off within seconds.

He could barely breathe as her hands ran over his chest and stomach. He kissed her neck again, then moved to her collarbone. He knew if there was a paradise, it could never match up to holding Cora in his arms and kissing her warm skin.

The bed shifted, and at first Leo thought it was from their weight, but then the bed frame cracked, and the mattress sagged. The sound of a torrent of water seemed to be coming from beneath the floor.

"Leo," Cora gasped. "The tremors have started."

He looked up to see a crack make its way down the stone wall. He pushed up from Cora, staying on the bed to protect her but keeping watch at the same time.

"What are the tremors? Like an earthquake?"

"Yes," she said, her eyes widening as another crack split down the wall. "This is a lot worse than the last time."

"Last time? What's going on?" Leo asked.

Cora sat up and grasped Leo's arm. "The Underworld is self-destructing without a strong leader."

Leo moved off the bed and pulled Cora with him. "We're doing this now," he said. "We can't wait another moment."

She threw her arms about his neck, holding him tight, and Leo buried his face in her neck, inhaling her scent for what might be the last time.

"I'm so sorry," she said. Another rumble came from beneath their feet, shaking the ground so hard that they nearly fell.

Leo gripped her tighter. "I'm not," he replied. "If this is the only way, then this is what I want to do."

She pulled away from him just as the sound of her father's voice echoed through the corridor.

"Cora!" he was shouting.

Leo hurried to the door, Cora at his side. Just as they reached it, the Grim Reaper entered. He looked from Leo to Cora, then said, "The sacrifice needs to happen now."

Leo's stomach dropped, but there was no time to waste. He grasped Cora's hand as they followed her father along the red corridor. When they reached the central courtyard, there were dozens of reapers already there.

Their cloaked forms reminded Leo of a plague of rats. Some of them were on the ground, as if they had been injured and were in pain. Others clustered together as if they were trying to find protection from the destruction rampant around them. The cracked ground was wet with the spilled water from the Fountain of Youth.

Cora's grip tightened on his hand, and he could almost feel her heart racing.

"I've brought the sacrifice!" she called out over the rumbling ground and reapers' cries.

The noise intensified, and sound seemed to be coming from everywhere at once. Leo wasn't entirely sure if it was from the reapers or from the echoing ground.

Cora brought him to a stop in front of the fountain where the Grim Reaper was standing, his shoulders hunched, his face pale.

The Grim Reaper wrenched Leo's arm behind his back with tremendous strength, so that even if Leo had been prepared, he felt weak in comparison. Then the Grim Reaper tied Leo's wrists together with some material that held fast.

Next, the Grim Reaper grasped Leo's upper arm and tugged him onto the low stone wall. All the reapers had turned their attention to him by now. The Grim Reaper forced Leo to his knees, and his skin scraped against the stone. His skin flashed between hot and cold, and Leo felt completely exposed with his bare torso decorated only by the jeweled necklace.

Cora raised her scythe to shoulder level, and silence descended like a billowing cloak. Her dress glowed red amid the dust from the crumbling stone. For a moment, there was no sound, but then the ground started to groan again. "With this sacrifice, I become the queen of the Underworld," Cora called out. "And all subjects will bow down to me in obedience. We will reunite and restore order to earth."

The din became deafening with both approving chants and dissenting cries.

Cora turned toward Leo, and he saw the tears streaking her face as she lifted the scythe over her head, then swung it toward him.

Twenty

The reapers are chanting around me, filling the courtyard space with their voices. The cries of "Kill him! Kill him!" separate from the crowd and join together, as if I need to be urged on.

My stomach feels upside-down, and I want to sink to my knees and keen.

Leo's dark, wavy hair has fallen out of its tie, and his shoulders and chest gleam with perspiration. The jewels upon his neck that give him protection against aging rapidly in the Underworld now glimmer in mockery.

If only the necklace could protect him from me.

But I cannot fail my father or my realm.

Ever since meeting Leo, my existence has changed. I have been living inside an alternate reality. I have felt the passions of mortals and known love. I have also come to know that sorrow can run deeper than I ever thought possible.

For Leo's gaze upon me makes me want to renounce everything that I am and ever will be in order to spare him this act.

With the scythe raised over my head and the reapers' cries blending with the groaning of the Underworld, I make the only decision I can. I swing the blade, strong and sure, toward Leo's neck.

He closes his eyes, but I cannot. Part of my penance will be to never forget what I have done and the price that we will both pay. Leo with his life, me with my heart.

The blade connects with a crack against his skin and bones. But instead of losing his head, he is flung to the ground with the force of the blow. The side of his head smacks against the stone, but it's still intact.

The reapers fall silent in an instant.

I stare at Leo's body as every part of me trembles with shock.

There is a thin line of blood between his shoulder and neck, as if I'd only grazed him with a small hunting knife.

The blood slowly beads and collects into a drop, and I watch as the drop of blood makes its way across his chest. The drop travels until it can no longer use his chest as a trail and finally releases and falls to the ground.

As it hits the stone beneath Leo's body, the ground stops shuddering. And all the reapers fall to their knees. The place is so quiet that I can hear only my rapid breathing.

I cannot take my eyes from Leo, for I realize he is still alive.

How did my blade not slice clean through his neck?

And how is he still breathing after such a blow? I look at my father, and he appears to be dumbfounded as well. He is staring down at Leo with an expression of incredulity.

The reapers are not moving. It's as if everyone is transfixed on the prince laying across the stone wall.

Then, as if the vast room has been dipped in colored dye, the ground crystallizes to golden yellow and grows smooth. The entryways of the corridors beyond the fountain shine with luster and strength. And the stones of the fountain bleach silver with black marble threads.

I feel as if I've lifted from the ground and stepped into the vortex. But there is no gray here. The colors are brilliant. The dark blue of Leo's pants contrast against the soft gray stone beneath him. His torso is golden, not the pale blue of a dead man. The fountain water bubbles with a translucent rainbow of colors.

Even the reapers seem to have brighter countenances.

And my father... I look at him. His eyes are the same black, and his skin is still pale, but he has stopped trembling.

One of the reapers cries out, "Look!"

I look down at Leo. His eyes are blinking open, his lips have parted, and his chest and shoulders rise with his breathing.

He is alive. Truly alive.

Panic darts through me. I've not done my job. I've not...

"He is immortal!" another reaper says.

And then I see it. His skin has smoothed, and his scars are gone. Any imperfections of his mortal body have disappeared. The color of his eyes is still a deep blue, but there is an eternal depth to them now.

I sink to my knees next to him. "Leo," I whisper. "What has happened?" I touch his face, hardly believing that he's alive after I struck him with the scythe. Leo watches me with a dazed expression as if he can't quite believe he is alive either. The thin cut on his neck is already healing—is this why he's alive? Because I somehow didn't use all my strength? Or . . . my gaze moves to the jeweled necklace.

I drop my hand, still staring at him. I do not understand fully, but it must have something to do with the jewels. I look up to my father, and I see the triumph in his eyes.

"You knew?" I ask.

"I hoped." His answer is simple, yet says so much.

The reapers are still kneeling, their heads bowed in respect. I look over the mass of subjects and find no defiance. Whatever has happened has been enough. The ground has stopped shaking, the walls have stopped crumbling, and the very atmosphere feels strong and energetic and living. As if the Underworld is healing itself.

Leo pushes himself up to his elbow, and the movement draws my attention again.

His deep blue eyes scan my face, searching for what? I don't have answers, and I feel my skin warm beneath his scrutiny.

"I feel different," he says in a quiet voice, an almost teasing tone.

"You are . . . *immortal*." The word on my lips is something I thought I'd never say to him.

One side of his mouth lifts in a tender smile, and then he grasps my hand and brings it to his lips. After pressing a kiss on the back of my hand, he says, "I'm here to serve you, my queen."

My heart feels as if it might burst out of my chest.

I rise to my feet, his hand still in mine, and I help him stand. He doesn't need help, though, as it turns out. He is stronger than before. Stronger than ever. His appearance is still the same, that of a man in his late twenties, but there is nothing mortal about him now.

My father moves away from the fountain and lifts his hand to command attention from the reapers. "You have paid your respect to our new queen," he says in his deep voice. "You will now return to your duties with all haste."

A murmuring among the reapers arises—not one of dissension, but one of strategy and commitment. Groups of reapers move to the portals, and one by one, they transport to earth. Soon the courtyard is quiet again, and the only sound is the bubbling of the fountain.

I can't stop staring at Leo. I want to touch him to see if he is real. But I already know, although I am still comprehending.

"Did you know about this too?" I ask him in a quiet voice, daring him to admit it.

His gaze flicks to my father, then back to me. I know without his answer.

"We thought it was a possibility," Leo finally says. "I'm pleased it worked." He touches the necklace. "Your father recommends that I keep this on."

I want to laugh with relief, with pure joy, but instead the tears build in my eyes, burning hot. "I don't know if I should banish you for not telling me or kiss you."

He smiles a full smile and takes a small step toward me, and I know my answer.

Before I can make the first move, he pulls me into his arms. And there, in front of my father, the Grim Reaper, Leo kisses me.

I melt into his embrace, feeling as if I've just entered the most glorious and delicious dream. Leo is alive, he's immortal, and I am his queen. I kiss him back as I wrap my arms about his neck and bring him even closer until there is no space between our bodies.

Kissing Leo is different this time. Not because he's immortal, but because this time I know he is mine. Truly. And forever.

About Jane Redd

Writing under Jane Redd, Heather B. Moore is a *USA Today* bestselling author. She writes the young adult speculative series *Solstice* under Jane Redd, and historical thrillers under the pen name H.B. Moore. Her latest thrillers include *Slave Queen, The Killing Curse,* and *USA Today* bestseller *Poetic Justice.* Under the name Heather B. Moore, she writes romance and women's fiction; her newest releases include the historical romance *Love is Come.* She's also the coauthor of the *USA Today* bestselling series Timeless Romance Anthology.

For book updates, sign up for Heather's email list: hbmoore.com/contact

Website: HBMoore.com
Facebook: Fans of H.B. Moore
Blog: MyWritersLair.blogspot.com
Instagram: @authorhbmoore
Twitter: @HeatherBMoore

www.ingramcontent.com/pod-product-compliance
Lightning Source LLC
LaVergne TN
LVHW021822060526
838201LV00058B/3478